LANDSLIDE

Frank raced down the mountain slope, weaving through the trees, as Joe trailed behind him. When Frank emerged, he hesitated for a moment before heading to the right.

Suddenly Frank felt the ground start to give way under his feet. He threw his arms back and tried to catch on to something, but there was nothing to grab.

"Help!" Frank cried, his arms frantically windmilling. Then as he lost all control, helpless panic overtook him, and he plunged down a crevice.

At the sound of Frank's voice, Joe stopped dead in his tracks. "Frank! Where are you?" Joe shouted, but he received no answer. Joe scrambled toward the direction where Frank's voice had come. As he approached two enormous rock slabs, Joe spotted an opening between the rocks.

Joe peered down through the gap and gasped. Fifteen feet below, his brother was lying in a heap, his eyes closed and his shirt bloody.

Books in THE HARDY BOYS CASEFILES® Series

Available from ARCHWAY Paperbacks

THE HARDY BOYS NO. 75
CASEFILES

NO WAY OUT

FRANKLIN W. DIXON

EAU CLAIRE DISTRICT LIBRARY

AN ARCHWAY PAPERBACK
Published by POCKET BOOKS
New York   London   Toronto   Sydney   Tokyo   Singapore

AN ARCHWAY PAPERBACK *Original*

An Archway Paperback published by
POCKET BOOKS, a division of Simon & Schuster Inc.
1230 Avenue of the Americas, New York, NY 10020

Copyright © 1993 by Simon & Schuster Inc.
Produced by Mega-Books of New York, Inc.

ISBN: 0-671-73111-4

First Archway Paperback printing May 1993

10 9 8 7 6 5 4 3 2 1

THE HARDY BOYS, AN ARCHWAY PAPERBACK and colophon are registered trademarks of Simon & Schuster Inc.

THE HARDY BOYS CASEFILES is a trademark of Simon & Schuster Inc.

Cover art by Brian Kotzky

Printed in the U.S.A.

IL 6+

Chapter

1

"AMAZING, HUH?" Frank Hardy said, squinting against the bright sunlight of Sun Valley, Idaho. "Twenty-four hours ago we were watching TV indoors in Bayport, and now I feel as if I could bump my head against the sky."

"I hope not," his brother, Joe, said with a laugh. "We haven't even started hiking up yet." The blond, muscular seventeen-year-old inhaled the crisp air of the Pioneer Mountains and gazed up at the pine-covered peaks surrounding them. Down on the lower slopes it was a warm May afternoon, but some of the higher peaks were still topped with patches of snow.

"How many times do we have to tell you, Joe," a voice cut in impatiently, "we're not going hiking. Rob's sport is called orienteering, and we'll never get to try it if you stand around gawking all day."

Joe turned to watch athletic Liz Webling climb out of the four-wheel-drive station wagon they had arrived in. She was followed by Frank's girlfriend, Callie Shaw, and Callie's friend Rob Niles. "Right, Ms. Investigative Reporter," Joe said dryly. "I forgot—you have a story to write."

"You bet," Liz said as she and the other two joined the Hardys. "And, I hope, a hard course to run." A reporter for the Bayport *Times,* the newspaper her father owned in Bayport, Liz was writing a story about orienteering. She and Joe enjoyed teasing each other, but Joe knew that the attractive teenager was as excited as he was to be there. Her hazel eyes sparkled beneath her short, neatly cut hair.

"For us, it will be hard, believe me." Dark-eyed Callie linked her arm with Frank's. "I've been reading about orienteering in Rob's letters ever since he went off to college. He makes it sound like the world's most demanding sport."

"I don't mean to," Rob protested with a laugh. Unlike the others, who were dressed in jeans, short-sleeved shirts, hiking shoes, and backpacks, Rob wore a thorn-resistant orange nylon jumpsuit, a small black waist pouch, and rubber-studded sneakers. On anyone else the out-

2

fit would have looked weird, Joe decided, but Rob's easygoing manner helped carry it off.

"All you have to do is race through the woods from one checkpoint to another, using only a special map," Rob explained to Callie. "The best part about it is that anyone can win—all you have to do to win is cross the finish line first."

"I've seen one of those orienteering maps, and I think it just looked like a series of squiggles and circles," Liz protested. "Not all of us have the brains to be a national champion like you. I heard you have to be a genius to win."

"Hardly a genius," Rob said modestly, running a hand through his dark, curly hair. "But it doesn't hurt to know when to cut across a valley instead of following it, or to hike straight up a mountainside instead of going around it. Some people you can outmuscle, but there's always some super-fit athlete you can beat only by outthinking."

"That's what I mean," Liz said eagerly. She pulled a small notebook from her shirt pocket and referred to it. "That's why they call orienteering the thinking sport." When Rob stared at her curiously, she admitted, "I read up on it after Callie invited me on this trip."

Callie laughed, and Joe saw her exchange a knowing smile with Frank. Callie had been friends with Rob when he was still at Bayport High winning relay races. She'd kept up her friendship with him now that he was in college. The spring before Rob had helped his team at Idaho State University win the national championship in orienteering and broke the collegiate orienteering record at the same time. This year Rob had asked Callie and her friends to join him for some warm-up racing two weeks before the national meet in Colorado. Callie had told the Hardys she was sure Liz and Rob would hit it off.

"Enough talking," Rob said easily. "Let's get going."

"I don't see the course," Joe protested as Rob led the way toward the forest. "And where are our maps? Are we the only people running this course?"

"Hold your horses," Rob said over his shoulder as he passed into the forest and started up the gently sloping base of the mountain. Joe spotted a small yellow metal triangle nailed to a tree and saw that Rob was following a path of sorts. "This is a practice course, and we do have maps. I picked them up for us at the hotel. This Sunday we're going to enter a real meet in the Sawtooth National Recreation Area near here. I need to run it as a training exercise, but you can enter it for fun."

"Whew! I'm bushed already," Callie said as they reached a small clearing several hundred yards above the road.

"Don't worry," Rob said with a wide grin.

"You won't start racing right away. First you have to learn the rules."

They all listened as Rob described his sport. "Think of an orienteering course as a golf course, with markers laid out like the flags at the golf holes. Only our flags happen to be hidden in the wilderness. Each runner carries a scorecard, and when he reaches a flag, or control point, he punches his card with a special holepunch. That's how he proves he made it to that checkpoint."

"So the first person to make it through all the checkpoints, in sequence, wins, right?" Frank said.

"Right," Rob echoed. "Now I'll show you the map for this course." He removed two small maps from his pouch and unfolded one on the ground. They all gathered around to examine it.

"Sun Valley is a two-point-five-mile course." Rob ran his finger over the series of irregular-shaped circles moving out from the center of the page like ripples in a pond. The circles were covered with splotches of color and a number of mysterious symbols. "The different colors mark depressions, dense vegetation, and cleared areas," Rob explained. "The triangles and squares stand for landmarks—like large boulders or buildings. The red circles with the numbers inside them are the control points. Orienteering meets are held in different places every time, so the only way to plan a route is to study the map right before the race starts."

Joe frowned. The topographical map looked to him like the scribblings of a two-year-old. "I don't see how you can read this and run through the woods at the same time," he said.

"It takes some getting used to," Rob admitted. "Once you get the hang of it, though, it's really fun." Rob handed Frank a compass and a scorecard from his pack. "The start is over there, between those two big trees. You guys start figuring out your route. I'll give you advice if you need it."

Excited by the challenge, Joe led the others up the slope where he spotted a small stake with a yellow triangle nailed to it. "I found it!" he shouted, feeling as proud as if he'd tracked down his first control point. He stopped to consult the map he was holding. "I think we just head off that way," he said, pointing to the right.

"Shouldn't we check the compass to get our bearings first?" Frank suggested.

"Besides, isn't that a creek right in our path?" Callie pointed out the thin blue line on the map off to their right.

Joe squinted at the squiggles and circles. "Okay, okay," he said impatiently, "but if we waste too much time reading the map, it'll slow us down."

"But if we start running before we read it, we won't make it through the course at all," Frank pointed out as he took the map.

"I think we'd better head northeast," Rob said, jumping in after checking his compass and map. "It means a pretty steep climb to get to the first few control points, but we'll bypass the worst of the creek. We should have a great view of that lake, too."

Joe stared at the map, trying to figure out what lake Rob was talking about. By then Rob had already loped off into the forest, with Liz right behind him. "We'd better go," Frank said to Joe and Callie. "We could end up lost if we don't follow Rob to the first flag."

As they ran, Joe tried to compare the scenery around him with what he had seen on the map. All he saw, though, were pine trees spreading out in all directions. Besides, he needed all his concentration just to pick his way through the branches and undergrowth.

A few minutes later Joe felt completely lost. He shook his head, wondering how long it would take for him to connect the map to the real world.

"All right!" Joe heard Liz's high voice cut through the still mountain air. "We found it!"

A moment later the Hardys and Callie emerged from the dense cover to see Liz and Rob beside a red and white flag in the center of a tiny clearing. Rob was showing Liz how to punch the scorecard.

"Now all you have to do is find fifteen more flags like this one," Rob told them with a smile. "And practice until you get superfast."

"Shouldn't you be practicing with your team?"

7

Liz asked as they strolled to the edge of the clearing.

"Our coach has scheduled a team workout in Colorado a few days before the nationals," Rob explained. "The rest of the time I find I focus better on my own." Rob rounded a large boulder, disturbing a chipmunk before he and Liz set off running again.

"Looks as if Rob's found a captive audience," Frank said as he, Joe, and Callie consulted their map.

"I know why," Callie said. "That dark, curly hair, those dimples—Rob's pretty cute."

"Hey, wait a minute," Frank said. "One fan is enough."

Callie smiled, her blond hair swinging. "Don't worry," she said, staring at Frank. "I like the view from here."

Joe frowned impatiently. "I'd like to see the view from the next checkpoint, if the two of you don't mind."

Frank laughed. "We're coming," he said.

Just past the first control point, the trail became steeper, with large, jagged rock formations jutting out all around them. Shrubs poked out from between cracks in the rocks, and trees grew between them at odd angles. Joe wiped the sweat from his face, silently wishing he hadn't given up running every day back in Bayport. Finally he, Frank, and Callie caught sight of Liz and Rob. Joe watched as Rob carefully picked his way around the imposing rocks. Clearly he hadn't found the second marker yet.

Joe climbed up to a ledge several yards above Rob and Liz. The ledge was about ten feet across and curved around the side of the mountain. The rocky mountain wall that rose above the ledge was studded with small trees and enormous boulders.

Rounding a curve Joe spotted a flash of red and white stuck between two rocks on the ledge. "I found it!" he shouted.

"I'd like to thank all the little people who made this possible," Joe announced as he punched their scorecard a few moments later. His joke was interrupted by a strange clicking.

"What's that?" Callie asked. Joe looked down to see a handful of pebbles land at his feet. "Is someone—"

Before Callie could finish her sentence, Joe heard a louder rattling sound from above them. He dropped the holepunch and squinted up the mountainside. More pebbles were raining down on them from a ledge higher up. As he watched, the pebbles grew larger, and then Joe became aware of an ominous rumbling sound.

"What is it, Joe?" he heard Liz say behind him. Joe continued to stare up at the other ledge as several medium-size rocks bounded down toward them. Suddenly he sprang into action.

"Duck!" he yelled. "It's a rock slide!"

Chapter

2

FRANK STARED in disbelief as a rock storm ricocheted down the stone wall toward them. To his horror he spotted an enormous gray boulder teetering on the edge of the upper ledge. "Duck!" he heard Joe shout again. Frank spun around in time to see his brother knocking Liz to the ground where their ledge met the mountainside. Frank grabbed Callie by the arm and slammed her flat against the mountain as the boulder started to tip over the ledge.

"It's going to hit us!" Callie screamed as Frank flattened himself against Callie to protect her. They were directly under a small outcropping of rock.

Rob hit the wall beside Frank and Callie as a

gray stream of rocks—large and small—poured onto the outcropping and bounced out into space. The boulder hit the wall with earthshaking force just above them. Frank watched amazed as it bounced off, then sailed over the ledge and hurtled into the forest below. As it crashed through the trees, a second, smaller boulder bounced over the outcropping in its wake.

A brief downpour of smaller rocks followed. Then, as suddenly as it had begun, the deafening noise ceased. "Is it over?" Frank asked tentatively, sticking his head out.

"Watch out," Rob commanded sharply. "These slides are unpredictable. Rocks could have built up behind another of those large boulders and be pushing it down on us right now."

"I don't see any more big rocks up there," Frank said, peering up through the cloud of dust rising from the mountainside. A few small stones still trickled down, sliding onto the ledge around his feet. When Frank looked up at the ledge from which the boulder had fallen, he saw that its lip had broken off. It was now lying in jagged chunks on the ground below.

Just then Frank heard a low moan to his left. "Frank," called Liz. "Over here!"

Frank moved to a niche in the rock wall where Joe and Liz had found shelter. Liz was squatting beside Joe, who sat with one leg stretched out straight in front of him. "He twisted his ankle getting me out of the way," she explained to Frank. "I don't know if he can walk."

"Sure I can." Joe grimaced as he felt his ankle. "I just strained it a little, that's all. Help me up," he said to Frank.

Frank frowned, but he bent to support his brother. "Take it easy," he said, helping Joe to stand. "Maybe you should just rest here for a while."

"I'm okay," Joe insisted. He put his weight on his hurt leg, only to collapse with a groan.

"Joe, are you okay?" Callie's voice rang out. She and Rob joined the others.

"He twisted his ankle, and he won't admit he needs help walking. It's his Mr. Stubborn act," Frank said, annoyed. "He ought to win an Oscar."

"He ought to get something for saving me," Liz put in. "I can only imagine what would have happened to me if Joe hadn't done something." She pointed to a small swatch of red sticking out from beneath a pile of rocks. It was all that was left of the flag marking the second control point.

"Why on earth would they put a flag in a rock slide area?" Liz said, shaking her head in disgust.

"I don't think it is one," Rob said. "The map doesn't indicate this as a dangerous area. We might expect a slide if there had been a storm or some really dry weather. But we haven't had either of those lately."

"Guess we were just lucky," Joe said. He

stood up again and gingerly tested his ankle. This time he stayed on his feet. "Maybe we should go up to where it started and see if we can figure out what caused it."

"Okay," Rob agreed. "We'll have to go around the side, though, so we won't be climbing through the slide area."

"Can you make it, Joe?" Frank asked.

Joe limped around in a circle, then nodded. "I'm not going to set any orienteering records, but I can keep up."

After wiping the dirt and sweat from their faces and taking a drink from their water bottles, the five of them slowly climbed the steep, rock-studded slope. The group fell silent as their breathing became labored. Frank glanced back at Joe, who was working hard to keep the pressure off his ankle. Frank worried that his brother could seriously hurt his leg just trying to keep up.

The sun was sinking lower in the sky, but Frank could still feel its heat on the top of his head. When they reached the upper ledge, Rob stopped, pointing down. "There," he said. "You can see the rock pile."

"That boulder must have been right near here," Frank said, kicking at the dirt near the break in the ledge.

"Right," Rob said. "But what started it rolling?"

Before Frank could answer, he heard Joe say from behind him, "Hey—what's this?" Frank turned to see Joe sitting with his back against the mountain, while Callie and Liz took pictures of the magnificent scenery. Joe had picked up something, which he was turning over in his hands.

"What is it?" Rob asked.

"A blue plastic sun visor." Joe read the words printed across the front band: "Sun Valley Sportcenter. Idaho's Largest Full-Service Sporting Goods Store."

Rob said, "Somebody must have dropped it."

Frank took a closer look at the visor. Joe looked up at his brother. "Maybe whoever it was accidentally set off the slide," Joe speculated.

"That's a big 'maybe,'" Frank replied. "Besides, why wouldn't the person have called out a warning?"

Joe shrugged. "Maybe he couldn't see us. That visor looks new," he said. "It hasn't been out here long."

"Well, it doesn't do a lot for the scenery to have something like that lying around," Callie commented.

"We'll take it back down," Frank said. Joe nodded, already shoving the blue visor in his backpack.

"Maybe we should head back," Callie said. "How's your ankle, Joe?"

Joe struggled to stand. Putting weight on his left foot, he grimaced and said, "I hate to admit it, but it really hurts."

"You don't have to finish the course today," Rob assured him. "I never thought we would, actually. If we head down the mountain diagonally, we can be back at our car in no time and back at the hotel in less than an hour. We can always come back tomorrow—if Joe's ankle feels better."

"Great," said Liz, beaming at him. "Maybe tonight we could go out in Ketchum or Sun Valley. I need some local nightlife color for my article."

As the group moved slowly back down the mountain, Frank silently mulled over what could have caused the rock slide. He remembered the handful of pebbles that had scattered at their feet before the actual slide began. Then he remembered the way the boulder had teetered on the lip of the ledge. If a hiker had been up there leaning against the boulder, that could have caused the rock to slide. Then what had happened to the hiker? Wouldn't the person have stuck around to assess the damage?

Rob's unerring sense of direction led the group out of the forest and onto the narrow dirt road where Rob's station wagon was parked. The teenagers climbed in for the short ride to the small, three-story hotel in downtown Sun Valley, where they all were staying. The hotel catered to sports people, Rob had told them. In fact, since the Sawtooth meet was the only orienteering race in the state that weekend, Rob predicted that a few of his teammates would show up there.

"Boy, am I bushed," Joe announced to Frank as he collapsed on his bed in their second-floor room. The group had agreed to meet again after they'd cleaned up. "It's a good thing this hotel is used to hikers. They're going to find plenty of pine needles in my sheets."

Gently removing his left hiking boot and sock, Joe stared at his swollen ankle. "Ouch. That hurts," he remarked mildly.

"You really did twist it." Frank frowned. "You should put some ice on it."

"I think it'll be all right," Joe said. "Let's wrap it in the Ace bandage Rob gave us and forget about it. Anyway, I'm starved. Orienteering and rock dodging are hard work. Isn't Idaho supposed to have good potatoes or something?"

Frank skeptically raised an eyebrow at Joe. "You must have been paying attention in geography class."

Joe laughed. "Good. Let's go get some spuds, then."

The two showered and changed quickly. After wrapping Joe's ankle tightly, they headed to Rob's room in time to meet the girls outside his door.

"There you are." Rob opened the door wide to let the group enter. He had changed into black jeans, boots, and a starched white shirt.

Joe watched Liz's mouth drop open as she took him in and had to force himself not to laugh.

"The night life of Sun Valley awaits us," Rob said with a friendly wink at Liz. Turning to Joe, he added, "How's your ankle?"

"It's fine, but my stomach isn't. It's hollow." Joe followed Frank and the girls into the room.

"The food around here tends to be plain, but terrific, and lots of it. What do you have in mind?" Rob asked, closing the door.

"Burgers and fries."

Rob laughed. "I think we can accommodate you. Let's go."

Frank was turning back to the door when a slight movement caught his eye. Frank watched as a piece of paper was slid under the door.

"Hey, look." Pushing past the others, Frank picked up the folded piece of paper. "It's addressed to you," he said to Rob.

"What?" Confused, Rob took the paper from Frank and unfolded it.

"Read it," Joe said.

"I am." Rob squinted at the tiny piece of paper and read aloud slowly, " 'Orient yourself to a new sport.' " His eyes opened wide as he raised his head and added, " 'Because you're never going to make it out of Idaho.' "

Chapter

3

" 'NEVER GOING to make it out'?" Frank heard Callie repeat behind him. "Who could have left this?"

Frank jerked open the door and ran into the hallway. It was empty. With Joe close behind, he tore off down the hall toward the stairs.

Frank swung the door open and faced an empty stairwell. "You go up," he told Joe. Favoring his ankle, Joe took the stairs more slowly than Frank, who ran headlong down to the ground floor. When he opened the door, there was no one in sight.

"Anything?" he asked his brother when they met back up on the second floor.

Joe shook his head. "Not unless you're suspicious of an eighty-year-old woman looking for her grandson.''

"Who could have done this?" Frank asked Rob as they walked back into his room.

"And why?" Joe added.

Rob chuckled. "I was just telling Callie and Liz that it's probably one of my teammates playing a joke," he said with an easy shrug. "I figured some of the other guys might show up here this week. One of them's obviously trying to psych me."

"I don't get it," Joe said. "You call a death threat a joke?"

"What can I say? We 'o-ers' are a competitive bunch," Rob said. "Believe me, I've seen—and done—a lot worse."

"This," Liz said, shaking her head, "is going to be a great article."

Rob grinned at her. "I'm just glad Takashi isn't here. He might be good for your story, but he likes his pranks rough."

"Who's Takashi?" Callie asked.

"Takashi Okira," Rob said. "He's number two—after me—on my squad. We've been going at each other since I set the collegiate record."

"What do you mean—going at each other?" Joe prodded.

"It started with him short-sheeting my bed," Rob replied. "Then he set a few booby traps on the course. Then I poured shampoo into his

19

mouthwash bottle—they nearly hospitalized him when he started frothing at the mouth.''

Rob sighed and sat down in a chair near the window. ''Takashi started taking it too seriously, then. In a meet last fall he deliberately knocked me into a ditch. A spotter saw him, and he was disqualified. Our coach kicked him off the team for a month. Takashi was humiliated, and he's hated me ever since.''

''May I see the note?'' Frank asked.

''Sure.'' Rob held it out. ''I remember now— Callie told me you two are amateur detectives. But, like I said, this has to be a joke.''

Without answering, Frank took the note and examined it. ''Look.'' Frank ran a finger over the notepaper. ''The message was typed—probably on an electric typewriter—but underneath you can see the impression of some numbers. This note must have been under some other paper the typist wrote on.''

Joe grabbed a pencil from the bedside stand and lightly ran the side of the lead over the paper. ''Check it out,'' he said. ''They're phone numbers.''

Frank grabbed the phone. ''Maybe they'll give us a clue to who left the note.''

Frank dialed the first number, ignoring Rob's gentle laughter. ''No answer,'' Frank said, pressing the receiver button. ''Give me the second number.''

A moment later Frank hung up again. ''Same

thing. Do you mind if I keep the note, Rob? I want to try the numbers again later."

"In the meantime," Callie said after Rob had nodded his permission, "how about some dinner? All this drama has left me absolutely starved."

As the group headed downstairs, Frank thought about what Rob had told them. He knew about the practical jokes athletes played on one another and had even taken part in a harmless prank or two himself. He'd never heard of anyone threatening to kill a teammate, though.

Rob opened the stairwell door on the first floor, accidentally smacking someone standing behind it. "Whoops—sorry," Rob said, stopping abruptly.

"Watch it!" said the dark-haired young man. He turned to scowl at his attacker. When he saw Rob, his eyes widened.

"Takashi!" Rob exclaimed. "What are you doing here?"

"You!" Takashi's face clouded over. Frank noted that he was about Rob's age but was shorter and more muscular than Callie's friend. "I thought you'd duck the Sawtooth meet. Do I have to see you everywhere I go?"

"I'm just here to get in a little practice," Rob said. "Like you."

"It won't do you any good, Niles," Takashi sneered. "You're finished. And I'm your worst enemy, because I'm taking your number-one ranking."

Rob sighed. "Sure, Takashi. Whatever you say."

Takashi drew closer to Rob, his fists clenched into tight balls. As Frank started toward the two athletes, he heard a voice down the corridor call out sternly, "What's going on?"

Frank turned to see a tall, thin man with a graying beard striding toward the group. The man grabbed Takashi's upraised arm and said, "One more incident like this, and I'll suspend you from the nationals."

"There's nothing going on, Coach," Takashi said innocently. "Rob and I were just saying hello."

"Give me a break," the bearded man said. "How many times do I have to tell you—we're a team, remember? Especially in public," he added in a low voice, indicating the onlookers in the lobby.

Takashi threw up his hands and stomped off. "You're coach of the whole team, not just your 'star,'" he called over his shoulder.

Rob turned to the older man. "Sorry, Coach," he said. "I just didn't expect to see him here."

"I didn't, either," said the man. "He told me he was going to visit relatives in Arizona. Anyway, since he is here, I expect you two to get along."

Rob nodded. "Coach Santina, let me introduce you to my friends."

Frank, Joe, Liz, and Callie all shook hands with Rob's orienteering coach. Frank liked the man's friendly smile and the way he patted Rob proudly on the back. "If you kids are interested in orienteering, you have a terrific teacher right here," he told them. "He's one of the best players since the sport was invented in Sweden a hundred years ago."

"Orienteering started in Sweden?" Joe asked, surprised.

"That's right," Santina told him. "Believe it or not, they used to play it in the mountains on skis. Some people believe the map-reading skills the Scandinavians picked up helped them out-maneuver their enemies during World War Two."

Frank glanced at Liz, who was scribbling the coach's words in her notebook.

"Listen, I know I okayed your working out on your own for a few days," Santina said, turning to Rob. "But I started thinking about it, and I thought I'd come over to work with you a bit. You need to concentrate on hills. And a little more practice getting through technical control areas wouldn't hurt, either."

Rob nodded, listening carefully. "You got it," he said with a grin.

"You boys are the best," Coach Santina added. "The nationals are going to be tough, so I need to put in some extra work as well."

When the coach left, Rob told the group, "He's got to be a little nervous because we have a couple of mean contenders breathing down our necks."

"Can we finish talking while we eat?" Liz cut in.

"Good idea," Rob said. "It'll give me a chance to catch up on the news in Bayport. And," he said, smiling at Liz, "to find out more about all of you, too."

The next morning Joe sleepily followed his brother into the hotel lobby. After a long, laugh-filled dinner, the Hardys had stayed up late talking about the rockslide, the note, and Takashi Okira. Despite Rob's assurance that the note was a psych job, the Hardys were worried. Before they fell asleep, they agreed to find out more about Takashi Okira.

"Whose idea was it to meet at nine?" Joe grumbled as the brothers picked out Liz, Callie, and Rob from among the groups of backpackers lingering near the lobby doors.

"You were the one who mentioned early birds and worms over burgers last night," Liz remarked.

"Once we get out on this orienteering course, you'll be glad you got up early," Rob assured Joe. "We're going to the Sawtooth National Recreation Area. Actually, we're late. Two other guys from my team checked in last night, and they're out running already. Come on, we'll grab some breakfast on the way."

"Breakfast." Joe's expression brightened. "At

least my ankle's better," he announced, as he followed Liz and Rob out of the hotel.

Rob and Liz paid no attention as they hurried to Rob's car. Frank and Callie strode after them, their arms around each other's waist. Joe let them pass. Everyone was paired off except him. Just then he glanced up and saw a beautiful, dark-haired girl in shorts and a red windbreaker running toward him.

"Hey, wait for me!" the girl shouted. Joe stopped in his tracks and waited for the girl to catch up. As she got closer, Joe noticed her big brown eyes, long dark hair, and perfect white smile. Suddenly he felt great.

"Sylvia!" Rob said, startled. "What are you doing here?"

The girl stopped short and stared at Rob. "That's nice. I haven't seen you for three weeks, and all you can say is, 'What are you doing here?' "

"Sorry," Rob said. "I-I'm just surprised." He moved toward Sylvia and gave her a quick hug. Liz stepped back. "These are friends of mine from Bayport," Rob said. "Frank and Joe Hardy, Callie Shaw, Liz Webling—this is my, uh, friend—Sylvia Rivera."

"Nice to meet you all," Sylvia said, then quickly focused on Rob. "I thought I was your *girl*friend."

"Nice to meet you, too," Liz said.

Joe realized Liz was as disappointed as he

25

was. To give her time to recover, Joe asked Sylvia, "Out for a morning jog?"

"I'm staying at a bed-and-breakfast up the road with some sorority sisters," Sylvia replied, giving Joe a big smile. "I decided to run down this way so I could see Rob. I thought maybe we could get a bite to eat."

"Whoa, wait a minute," Rob said with a hint of irritation. "You didn't even tell me you were coming."

"I *thought* I'd surprise you. I *thought* it'd be a nice surprise," Sylvia said in a tight voice.

"Oh, it is. It is," Rob said tensely. "But I can't eat breakfast with you. We're about to do some o-ing so Liz can write about it for her newspaper back home."

Liz smiled weakly. "Why don't you join us? We'd love to have you come."

Sylvia stared at Liz suspiciously. "No, thanks," she said. "Rob, can I speak to you a minute? Alone?"

Sylvia and Rob moved a few steps away to talk. Two minutes later Sylvia turned and began running down the road again.

"I take it Sylvia's not coming with us," Joe said.

"No," Rob replied. "Sylvia and I broke up a few weeks ago," he explained. "But she's still a little—well, possessive."

"Why did you break up?" Liz asked.

"We'd been dating on and off for a couple of

years," Rob said. "She used to be a top o-er, but now she says she's sick of it. That doesn't make our relationship any easier. Neither does the fact that I can't take her to her sorority's spring formal because of the nationals." He seemed to be lost in a reverie for a moment. "Well, enough soap opera," he said. "Let's go run Sawtooth."

As they drove past the sign announcing Sawtooth National Recreation Area, Callie said, "I don't think they need a sign to tell us we've arrived. This is spectacular!" Everyone agreed as the beauty of the mountain scenery unrolled before them.

"There are quite a few courses laid out in this area," Rob explained. "The Idaho Orienteering Club has set up some for beginners and a few others that are considered tough. There are certain areas I'm not allowed in."

"Why not?" Liz asked.

"This is where Sunday's race will be held," Rob said. "The area where that course has been set up is off limits to competitors."

A few minutes later Rob parked in a clearing beside the road. "A few different courses start around here," he said. He pulled out a map and pointed to a section marked by a little flag. "I'd like to try this one because it'll give me the right kind of workout. There's also a beginner's course that starts from here."

27

Rob pointed to another little flag on his map. "Here's a map and compass. You guys can see how much map reading you learned yesterday."

"Great," Frank said. "We can meet back here when we're finished."

The two groups split up, Liz and Callie going with Rob to the start of his course. Frank and Joe headed out in another direction. Their starting point was at the base of a steep slope. Patches of snow dotted the upper elevations of the mountainside.

"Let's go," Joe said, starting up the slope.

"Just a minute." Frank grabbed his brother's arm. "You want to tell me where you're going?"

"Well, I thought we'd start here at this circle numbered *1*," Joe suggested.

"Very helpful," Frank said, rolling his eyes.

Consulting the compass and orienting the map to the surrounding terrain, Joe led the way up the mountain and through the scattered pines, logs, and rocks to the first checkpoint. Then, after much wandering, they found the next. Frank was relieved to see that signs had been placed at certain points, warning o-ers not to stray too far afield.

As they panted up a steep slope, attempting a shortcut through the forest, Joe asked, "Did Sylvia strike you as the jealous type?"

Frank let out a laugh. "She didn't seem happy to see Rob enjoying Liz's company."

"That's what I thought." Joe stopped and

turned to face Frank. "Do you think she's mad enough to threaten Rob?"

Despite the cool air at that high altitude, Frank felt overheated. "Do you think she wrote that note?" he asked Joe.

Joe shrugged. "I don't know. I don't know if she'd start a rockslide, either. It is interesting that she's here and that she's angry."

Frank nodded. "It might be worthwhile to find out if she has access to a typewriter," he said.

The two brothers climbed to the third control point. "It looks as if we have a downhill run, a creek, and some thick forest to the next checkpoint," Frank noted. The map was beginning to make sense to him.

"You're on," Joe said. "Ready?"

Frank nodded and off they went. With one eye on each other and one eye on the rugged terrain, they tore down the mountain slope.

Halfway down the slope Frank began to run outside the path he had marked for himself on the map. He wove among the trees, trying to keep the line of the creek in mind and his brother behind him. Emerging from a clump of trees, he hesitated for a moment before heading to the right and what he hoped was a clearing.

Suddenly Frank felt the ground start to give way under his feet. He threw his arms back, hoping to grab on to something, but there was nothing to grab.

"Hey!" Frank cried, his arms frantically windmilling. He dug in his heels and locked his knees, but still he continued to slide.

"Joe!" Frank yelled as he landed on his back and hurtled downward.

Helpless to stop himself, Frank felt a wave of panic wash over him. He was plunging down a crevice!

Chapter

4

"FRANK!" Joe called out as his brother disappeared from view. No answer came from him as Joe scrambled in the direction of Frank's voice. As he approached the place where two enormous rock slabs met, Joe spotted an opening between the rocks. It was hard to see at first because the nearer rock was higher than the other one. As Joe moved closer he saw that the gap was nearly five feet wide and the path down through it was littered with hundreds of loose stones and pebbles.

"Frank!" Joe shouted, peering down through the gap. His brother was lying in a heap fifteen feet below. Frank's eyes were closed and his shirt was torn. There was blood on the sleeve of his rugby shirt.

"Frank!" Joe shouted again. "Can you hear me?"

Slowly Frank's eyes opened. He looked up at Joe with a dazed expression. "I'm okay, I think." He cautiously moved his arms and legs. "No broken bones, anyway," he added sheepishly. "Watch out for that first step."

"Don't move," Joe called. "I'll find a way to lift you out."

Scanning the wooded area below the rocky slope, Joe spotted a tall blond man and a woman with a long dark braid jogging by in the distance. "Hey, up here!" he shouted, waving his arms. "Can you give me a hand? My brother's had an accident."

The couple slowed down and glanced in his direction.

"Up here!" Joe called again.

The pair stopped, and Joe watched as the man grabbed the woman by the arm and the two started to argue. Then all at once they took off.

"Hey, come back!" Joe yelled. "I need help!"

Bewildered, Joe turned back to the crevice. He saw that Frank had already made his way halfway up again.

"Hold on, Frank." Joe quickly lay across the rocks, one arm stretched down to his brother.

Thrusting himself up, Frank reached for Joe's

hand. Joe wrapped his hand around Frank's arm and pulled his brother up.

"Thanks, Joe," Frank said, lying flat on the rocky surface. "Give me a minute to catch my breath, and we'll head out of here."

"You sure you're okay?" Joe asked.

"Nothing a hot shower and a few Band-Aids won't fix, but I don't think even a good wash will save this shirt. Who were you yelling at?"

"A man and woman were jogging down below," Joe said. "I called for help, and they stood and talked, and then all of a sudden they ran away as though something had scared them."

"Like what?" Frank asked.

Joe shrugged. "We'd better head in. I hate to say it, but you blew our running time."

"I know. I was running too fast and didn't look where I was going," Frank admitted. "I guess Rob's right. This *is* a thinking sport."

Frank and Joe backtracked toward the marked trail. Nearly an hour later they reached their starting point to find Callie, Liz, and Rob waiting for them.

"What happened to you, Frank?" Callie called. "Did you fall off a cliff or something?"

"Or something," Frank told her sheepishly.

Joe laughed. "We're finding out that orienteering is a little tougher than we thought."

"I told you guys to take it slow," Rob said,

eyeing the blood on Frank's shirt. "Should we stop at a first-aid station?"

"I'm fine," Frank insisted. "How was your run?"

"It was great," Rob said. "Liz found two markers before I did. She and Callie are natural o-ers."

Liz smiled, a little embarrassed. "Let's get you back to the hotel, Frank," she said.

"Good thinking." Callie grasped Frank's hand firmly. "I think we've had enough for one day."

After the group had returned to the car, Callie turned to Rob. "Liz and I spent the whole run talking about orienteering. What are your plans after you graduate—pro o-ing?"

Rob grinned. "Actually, I've decided to head back home. I'm going to work in my dad's advertising agency."

"Are you majoring in advertising?" Frank asked.

"Yeah. I graduate in a couple of weeks," Rob answered. "I interned at my dad's firm the past two summers. In fact, he already has me penciled in to work on some of his biggest accounts, including the Freedom shoe line. Dad said he wants new blood on the project." Rob glanced at Liz's reflection in the rearview mirror. "Ad copy isn't as important as good newspaper writing, but it can be fun."

"Do you think you'll make it a career?" Liz asked.

"My dad thinks so," Rob said wistfully. "The only thing I know for sure is, I'm going to miss Idaho."

After a brief stop for Band-Aids, the group headed back to the hotel. After they entered the lobby, the friends split up to spend the rest of the afternoon on their own. Joe grabbed his chance to pull Frank aside. "Listen, I keep thinking about Sylvia suddenly appearing," he told his brother. "While you rest, I'm going to find the bed-and-breakfast where she's staying. Maybe I could look around for the typewriter that might have been used to write that note to Rob."

Frank nodded. "Good luck," he said with a weary sigh.

As Frank headed upstairs, Joe stayed in the hotel lobby and made his way over to a phone. Two hours later he still hadn't found Sylvia's bed-and-breakfast. He had made a dozen calls, and not one place had a Sylvia Rivera registered.

Joe was beginning to wonder whether he'd invented Rob's beautiful girlfriend when he recognized a tall man walking toward him through the front door.

"Coach Santina," Joe said, reaching out to shake the older man's hand. "I'm Joe Hardy, Rob's friend. I met you this morning."

The coach paused and smiled distractedly. "Oh, right."

35

Joe smiled. Coach Santina could probably tell him everything about Takashi Okira.

"Rob seems pretty excited about the nationals," Joe said casually. "Do you think he has a chance to repeat as national champion?"

The coach smiled. "Rob's still the best all-around o-er we have," he said, "but it's going to be a tough meet. Everyone's gotten better."

"What about Takashi?" Joe persisted, blocking Santina's path to the doors. "Do you think he can beat Rob?"

"When he's at his best, maybe," Coach Santina said, warming to his subject. He cocked his head philosophically and added, "Takashi's strength is his ability to concentrate. That happens to be Rob's greatest weakness. Once Rob's focus is blown, he tends to fall apart on the course. That's why Takashi constantly tries to psych him."

Joe acted confused. "I got the impression that the psych jobs were mutual," he said.

"Oh, they are," the coach agreed. "All the players play 'gotcha' with one another. Rob and Takashi's rivalry used to give them both an edge—but this year they've taken it way out of bounds."

Surprised, Joe started to ask what the coach meant by that, but Santina continued without pausing. "On the other hand, Rob's concentration has improved a little in the past month," he told Joe. "It was right that he broke up with that girl, Sylvia. They were always having flare-ups, and she demanded a lot of his time.''

Joe nodded politely as the coach glanced at his watch. ''I'm late for a training run,'' he said. ''Gotta go.''

''Thanks,'' Joe said. ''This is getting really interesting,'' he added to himself as the coach walked away. Joe stood and thought about what he had said. To Joe, it seemed equally likely—or, for that matter, equally unlikely—that either Takashi or Sylvia would have set off a rock slide and then slipped a threatening note under Rob's door. Who knows? he thought idly. Maybe Rob was right. Maybe the rock slide really was an accident of nature and the note just a sick joke of Takashi's.

He checked his watch. They were meeting again at six, and all he had learned that afternoon was that Rob had trouble concentrating and that Sylvia had probably lied when she said she was staying nearby. It wasn't much to go on. He headed back up to his room to report to Frank.

The boys joined their friends in the hotel lobby. They were going into Ketchum to O.J.'s Grill for dinner. Frank couldn't help but smile when he spotted Callie in her bright printed skirt and clean white blouse. Half a day of sun had given her skin a glow. She could have posed for an ad for good health.

"Feeling better?" she asked, taking his arm.

Frank glanced at Joe. The two of them had talked over Rob's predicament at length and had decided, for now at least, to play it cool and hope another clue surfaced soon. "I feel great," Frank replied. "I slept for a couple of hours."

They heard Liz ask Rob, "What kind of souvenirs do they sell in Idaho?"

"Potato paraphernalia," he answered with a laugh. "And for amateur o-ers, economy-size first-aid kits."

"Wow," Frank said twenty minutes later as he entered O.J.'s Grill behind Callie. The dimly lit restaurant had huge windows framing the magnificent mountains beyond. The sky was just beginning to darken but was still streaked with wild purples, pinks, and oranges.

"Isn't it romantic?" Callie whispered. "Liz and Rob certainly seem to like the atmosphere."

Frank glanced back at them. "I'm not sure they're noticing the scenery," he said with a laugh.

The food was as impressive as the surroundings. As they ate, Liz continued her cross-examination of Rob.

"If the Swedes did their orienteering on skis, when did people start running?" she inquired.

"Good question," Rob replied, "but I don't know the answer. But o-ers don't just ski or run, you know. In Japan they bicycle. In New York they use Rollerblades. I've even heard of people o-ing in wheelchairs."

"That's impossible!" Callie said, surprised. "How can they do that in the mountains?"

"You don't need mountains," Rob replied. "All you need is a compass and a map. There have been meets in San Francisco, in Caribbean coral reefs—even in suburban shopping malls. There's something about solving a puzzle while you run that appeals to the human mind," Rob added with a grin.

As they finished their desserts, Callie said to Rob, "Liz and I were thinking it would be fun to do some white-water rafting on the Middle Fork of the Salmon River. It's supposed to be the best rafting in Idaho, and it's only about fifty miles from here."

The rest of the group—including Rob— quickly agreed. With their plans set, the five friends headed back to the hotel. They agreed to turn in early so they could get an early start. In the lobby Frank, Joe, Liz, and Callie headed up. Only Rob lagged behind. "My dad said he'd call," he said. "I'm going to check at the desk for messages."

"Okay," Frank said. He and Joe walked Callie and Liz to their room.

Turning the corner into their own corridor a few minutes later, Frank spotted someone at the opposite end of the hall fiddling with the handle of a door near the stairwell. As the person opened the door and ducked into the room, Frank realized it was Rob.

"That's not Rob's room," Frank said, startled.

"Maybe he's visiting someone," Joe suggested.

"By sneaking in?" Frank said skeptically. "Let's check this out." Together, they crept down the hallway. Arriving at the room, Frank saw that the door was half open. He peered in, then stole in with Joe at his heels. As his eyes adjusted to the dark, Frank made out Rob's figure kneeling beside the nightstand.

"Rob," Frank whispered. "What are you doing?"

Rob jumped up with a gasp. "Frank! I—I was—" he stammered. Then he shrugged. "I was just playing a little trick."

"A trick?" Joe said. "On whom?"

"Takashi," Rob said, lowering his voice. "This is his room. I wanted to leave him a note like the one he left me. I'm just evening the score."

"Are you sure Takashi left that note?" Frank said.

"It couldn't have been anyone else," Rob insisted, his voice high and strained. "Look, he deserves a little of his own medicine."

Frank shook his head. "Won't your coach suspend you—after his warning this morning?"

"I guess you're right," Rob whispered. "Let's get out of here."

Joe turned and made his way toward the door,

with Frank and Rob just behind. How far, Joe wondered, were Takashi and Rob willing to go?

Joe crept to the doorway, his eyes trained on the shaft of light coming in through the crack. Suddenly a hand was thrust through the opening, thumping Joe in the chest.

"Wha—?" Joe cried in surprise. Before he could move, a man pushed into the room.

"Going somewhere, fellas?" a sarcastic voice asked.

Joe backed up. "Takashi!" he said.

Chapter

5

"LISTEN," Joe said, trying to sound light-hearted. "I know this looks bad, but we—"

Takashi laughed, but there was no humor in the sound. "Bad?" he said, switching on the overhead light. "Sure, it looks bad. What it looks like is that our Boy Wonder has lost his nerve and has to bring henchmen to do his dirty work."

"That's what I'm trying to tell you," Joe said, keeping his voice cool. "There *is* no dirty work."

"Right," Takashi scoffed. "I guess you three just like the view from my room so much you couldn't stay away."

Joe stepped toward Takashi. "We're only here because—"

Rob held his hand up to stop Joe. "I promise you, Takashi—no tricks, no games."

Takashi glared at his teammate silently for a moment. "You know, you're really too much, Niles," he said. "You expect me to believe you broke into my room to pay a social call? Give me a break. You're obviously trying to sabotage me before the nationals—"

"Look, you're jumping to conclusions," Frank interjected.

"Save it," Takashi snapped. "Maybe Coach Santina believes Rob's innocent act, but I don't. You guys make me sick," he added in a throaty voice. "Get out of here."

Rob threw up his hands. "If you're not going to listen, fine," he said. He walked through the doorway, with Frank following. Joe stood his ground. "Just wait a minute," he said to Takashi, trying to control his anger. "You think you can say whatever you want to people, but let me tell you something—"

"Joe," Rob said from the hallway in a tightly controlled voice, "let it go. We'll settle it at the nationals."

"Count on it!" Takashi cried, spinning around to glare at Rob.

Shaking his head, Joe left Takashi's room just before he heard the door slam loudly behind him.

"I can't believe we let that guy talk to us that

43

way," Joe said as they walked down the hallway toward Rob's room.

"Well, he did catch us snooping around his room," Frank reminded his brother. "Come on. Give the guy a break."

"I *was* planning some kind of psych job on him," Rob said. "It sounds pretty lame to say, 'Oh, yes, I had every intention of sabotaging you, but I just changed my mind.' I can see why Takashi wouldn't believe me."

"But it's the truth," Joe insisted. "And who knows what he'll tell your coach now."

Rob shrugged. "He won't tell him," he said confidently. They were at Rob's room. "Takashi and I have gotten into too much trouble from our little escapades. If he reports me, he could end up being suspended, too. Besides, Takashi wants to beat me, not get me thrown out."

Rob stepped inside, and Frank and Joe exchanged a glance behind his back. Joe knew Frank was thinking the same thing he was. Takashi might not report the break-in to Coach Santina, but he could decide to seek revenge some other way.

"The light's blinking on my phone," Rob said. "I guess there's a message for me after all."

Rob called the number for the front desk while Frank and Joe tiptoed through a maze of sneakers, T-shirts, and a wrinkled nylon jumpsuit to sit at a small table in a corner of the room.

"Help yourselves to juice and snacks in the fridge," Rob said.

Joe got up and rummaged through the refrigerator while Frank watched Rob depress the receiving button on the phone before beginning to dial again. "My dad left a message for me to call him," Rob said to him. "And Sylvia called, wanting to know where I was tonight," he added more quietly.

At the mention of Sylvia's name, Joe closed the refrigerator and turned to his brother. He handed Frank a bottle of juice and a bag of chips and nodded toward the sliding glass doors near the bed. "We'll give you some privacy," he said to Rob. Carrying a bottle of juice and some chips for himself, Joe led Frank through the doors onto a small balcony.

"So Sylvia's still around," Joe said to Frank as the older Hardy dropped into a patio chair and opened his bag of chips. The balcony overlooked a pool, which was surrounded on three sides by hotel rooms. The fourth side consisted of the hotel's lobby, with its restaurant and general store.

"We can only guess she's still around. She could have called the hotel from anywhere," Frank pointed out.

Joe sighed as he dropped into a chair beside his brother's. "I don't get it," he said, staring down into the deserted pool. "She said she was staying nearby, but I couldn't find her anywhere.

And she said she came to see Rob, but she hasn't turned up all day."

"Rob hasn't exactly been available," Frank reminded him. "In fact, it looks to me as if he's trying to avoid her." He sighed. "My guess is that Rob and Sylvia are stuck in one of those love-hate situations. He loves to be with her, but he hates the way she messes with his head."

"Hmmm." Joe frowned, munching on a chip. "The question is, how far will Sylvia go? She'd have to be awfully mad at Rob to roll a boulder down on him."

Frank was about to protest that they hadn't connected Sylvia in any way to the rockslide. In fact, they hadn't even tried to find the owner of the blue plastic visor. The door slid open then, and Rob poked his head out. "Hey, it's cold out there," he said. "Come on back in."

"So—what's up?" Joe asked casually. "Any news from your two phone calls?"

Rob stretched out on the queen-size bed as Frank and Joe returned to the table. "Well," Rob said, linking his hands behind his head, "I talked to my dad. It looks as if I'm going to be featured in a commercial."

"No kidding!" Joe said. "For what?"

Rob sat up, leaning against the pillows. "For orienteering. I told you about the big shoe account my dad's firm has been working on. The commercials for the shoes show young athletes wearing the shoes and talking about how great they are. Of course, they get paid for these little testimonials,'' Rob said, grinning.

"Anyway,'' he continued, "I've been trying to convince my dad that the commercials should include orienteering, since a lot of o-ers wear the company's trail-running shoe.''

"And let me guess,'' Frank put in. "He agreed to it, and now you're going to be the featured athlete,'' he said with a smile.

Rob turned to Joe. "He kind of takes the fun out of a big announcement, doesn't he?'' he said.

Joe laughed. "It's great news, anyway. What do you have to do exactly?''

"Dad said they'll take a few preliminary photos of me. The photos might give them ideas for the commercial. I guess I'm just supposed to do some o-ing with a photographer trailing me.''

"When do you start?'' Frank asked.

"Dad was surprised I hadn't started already,'' Rob said, raising his eyebrows. "He said they sent the account executive along with a photographer to meet me here. But I haven't heard from Jeremy yet.''

"Jeremy?'' Joe repeated.

"That's the account executive—Jeremy Foote. He's a rising star at my dad's company—a real go-getter,'' Rob said. "He started at the company seven years ago, right out of college, and he's been outhustling the competition ever since.

Last summer when I worked as an intern at the firm, I worked directly under Jeremy," Rob explained. "He taught me a lot."

Rob rearranged himself against the pillows and grinned. "If I know Jeremy, he's probably taking advantage of his trip to Idaho to spend time in the mountains. He loves the outdoors and takes at least one hunting trip every fall," Rob said. Then he stopped and looked up at the Hardys. "I'm not boring you, am I? I know it's no fun listening to someone talk about a stranger."

"No problem," Joe said, stifling a yawn, "but it is getting late. We should probably try to get some sleep."

Rob walked the Hardys to the door. "I want to thank you for trying to get me out of Takashi's room," Rob said. "He's not the only one who's gone too far, I guess. I don't need to blow my chances at the nationals, either."

Joe started to tell Rob it was nothing when a movement behind the athlete stopped Joe cold.

"Y-your bed," Joe stammered, staring past Rob. "Rob, look behind you—now."

"What's going on?" Frank demanded.

When Frank saw what Joe saw, he froze, too.

"What's up, guys?" Rob chuckled. "Did you see a ghost or s—"

As Rob glanced back at his bed, his words froze in his throat. The trio stared in shock as a long sinuous shape slid out from beneath the pillows Rob had been leaning against a few moments before. The shape moved down the bedspread, covering the mattress, and hesitated at the foot of the bed.

"Get back!" Rob yelled abruptly, throwing himself back against the wall. "That's a rattlesnake!"

Chapter

6

"IT'S OKAY, ROB," Joe said, grabbing the athlete by the shoulders. "We're right here. The snake isn't going to get you."

"I *hate* snakes!" Rob said, ignoring him. "I've always hated them. Whoever's out to get me knows that!"

Joe glanced at the bed and saw that Rob's shout had caused the four-foot snake to coil up at the foot of the bed. Its scaly skin was covered in a tan and brown pattern, and Joe could see the buttoned indentations of its rattle. The snake indicated that it had caught sight of Rob and the Hardys and began to turn its head toward them.

"I can't believe that thing was under the pillows while I was sitting on the bed."

Joe nodded. "We'll need a pole or a long stick and something to put the snake in."

"I'll get them," Rob said, backing out of the room. "Anything to get away from that thing."

Rob moved off down the hall and returned quickly with a broom. "I found this around the corner. Will it work?"

"Like a charm," Joe said. "And Frank took the pillowcase from the extra pillow in your closet."

Holding the broom by the bristles, Joe ventured back into the room, poking the pole toward the snake, which was wriggling on the bed, occasionally flicking its tongue. Joe tried to slide the pole under the snake. At first the snake slithered away, but then Joe finally got the broom handle under it and lifted it up. Beads of perspiration formed on his forehead as he kept his eyes trained on the rattler.

The snake wrapped itself once around the handle, and Joe slowly began moving the broom toward Frank, who was holding the pillowcase open beside the bed.

"Easy," Frank said. Joe kept his movements smooth as he swung the broom over the bed. The snake's rattle was still, and Joe didn't want his own nervousness to upset it. In one quick motion Joe dropped the broom handle inside the case, giving it a shake. Frank immediately closed the case around the handle, and Joe pulled the handle up through Frank's hands.

"Got him," Frank said, holding the squirming pillowcase. "Let's call an animal control agency and see if someone can pick this guy up."

Joe nodded as he watched relief spread over Rob's face. As Joe picked up the telephone directory from the nightstand, he noticed a folded piece of paper taped to the tabletop. "What's this?" he asked, pulling the paper away from the tape. Rob's name was typed on the outside.

Frank turned sharply to Joe as Rob said, "A note?"

Rob, still shaky from his encounter with the snake, opened it and read it out loud. " 'Snakes alive!' " he said. " 'Which is more than I can say for you if you don't get out of orienteering.' " With a somber expression, Rob handed the note to Joe.

"Same typewriter as the first note," Joe said grimly. "Even the same small notepaper."

"Whoever did this means business," Frank said, still holding the squirming pillowcase at arm's length.

"But how did that snake get in here?" Rob asked in a strained voice. "We've been here for the past fifteen minutes."

"Someone must have broken in just before then," Frank said as Joe called animal control. "When you got up off the bed, it must have felt the change in pressure and crawled out to see what was going on. It's a good thing you didn't go to sleep with it under there."

"Hey, Rob—who knows you're afraid of snakes?" Joe asked from beside the phone.

"Almost everyone," Rob said miserably, staying as far away from the pillowcase as he could. "I'm sort of known for it."

"I think it's time for us to go after the person doing this," Frank said. "Why don't we call that place that was advertised on that sun visor—that sporting goods store—and see if we can find out anything about it?"

"Good idea," Joe replied. "Remember we're going rafting, too, though. We should also try those phone numbers that we lifted from the first note." He didn't add out loud that he also wanted to talk to Sylvia Rivera. "If you don't mind, I'll keep this note, too. It could turn out to be evidence."

"Guys, this is great," Rob said weakly. "I know I laughed at you before for acting so suspicious, but now—well, I'm glad you're here."

At eight-thirty the next morning Joe answered a knock at his door to find Callie and Liz standing in the hallway, wearing shorts, T-shirts, and sunglasses.

"Good morning," Liz said cheerfully as the two girls stepped into the room. "Ready for rafting?"

"Come on in, but we'll have to whisper," Joe said. "Frank's on the phone."

Callie glanced from Joe to Frank. "What's going on?"

When Joe told them about the snake and the note in Rob's room, Callie said, "This is getting serious."

"I'll say," Liz added. "Is Rob okay?"

"Not bad, considering," a voice said behind her. Joe turned to see Rob standing in the doorway, a smile on his face. Joe was glad to see that the athlete did look more relaxed than he had the night before.

"It'll take more than a note—or even a snake—to get rid of me," Rob assured Liz as he entered the room.

Frank put the phone down as Rob closed the door. "Listen to this," he said excitedly. "Remember those numbers we found on the first note to Rob? I just called them. They were both for businesses, and they both were open. The first number is for a place called Mountain Mike's. It's a sporting goods store."

"I've heard of it," Rob said. "They sell a lot of fishing and hunting stuff."

Frank nodded. "And the second one," he said with emphasis, "is the number of Sun Valley Sportcenter."

Joe's eyes popped open. "The place the sun visor came from!"

"So it's off to Sun Valley Sportcenter?" Rob said, rattling his car keys.

"And then on to the Middle Fork," Liz replied, leading the group down to the lobby.

As they made their way by the front desk, Joe heard someone call out, "Rob!" Sylvia Rivera was striding toward the group. She had on denim shorts and a red T-shirt, and her long dark hair hung loose around her shoulders. She greeted Rob with a bright, steely smile that was more angry than happy and gave Liz an icy nod.

"Are you going somewhere?" Sylvia asked, taking Rob's arm.

Joe watched Rob force an awkward smile. "Well, uh—yeah," Rob stammered. Joe didn't know if Rob really disliked Sylvia, or just wanted to spend some time with his friends.

Liz quickly jumped in. "We're going rafting on the Middle Fork," she said, smiling at Sylvia. "Why don't you come with us? Six people is the perfect number for a raft."

"How do you know?" Joe said.

Liz glared at Joe, and Joe blinked, then turned to Sylvia. "Yeah, why don't you come? It'll be fun," he said. Besides, he realized, this could be his chance to cross-examine her.

A smile appeared on Sylvia's face. "Okay—that sounds good," she said, aiming the smile at Joe. "I'm ready when you are."

Everyone was quiet as they piled into Rob's station wagon and drove the short distance to Sun Valley Sportcenter, a huge sporting goods store that stood by itself on the highway up to the Middle Fork.

The group split into smaller groups to explore the store. Liz and Callie headed for the swimwear department while Sylvia and Rob wandered off to look at camping gear.

"Let's go," Joe muttered, guiding Frank to the large cashier's stand in the middle of the store. "I want to check out that visor before Sylvia gets back."

As they approached the cashier's stand, Joe spotted a young man standing in the stall whose name tag read Eric Ramirez—Manager. The man was dark-haired, solidly built, and, Joe guessed from the harried expression on his face, quite busy. Although the store had only just opened, a line of paying customers had already formed.

Joe removed the blue sun visor from the pocket of his windbreaker. "Excuse me," Joe said, "I found this visor a couple days ago, and I'm hoping to locate its owner."

Eric barely glanced at the visor. "It's ours," he said, "but we don't sell them. They're a promotional item. We give them out for free to anyone who asks about sporting events. If you attend an event in this area, we make sure Sportcenter is there with you," he rattled off in a tired voice.

"How long has the promotion been going on?" Frank asked.

"About two months," Eric said. "I don't

know how you could find out who that one belongs to. Anyway, I wouldn't worry about it."

"Thanks," Joe said as Eric turned away.

"Well, there goes that lead," Frank said as they left the checkout counter. "All we know is that somebody left it there within the last week or so."

"We still haven't talked to Sylvia," Joe pointed out stubbornly. "She could have typed those threatening notes in her hotel room, wherever that is. And from the expression on her face this morning, I'd say she'd be willing to put a dozen snakes in Rob's room."

Before Frank could answer, Rob approached them with a man who seemed to be in his late twenties. He was dressed casually in brand-new jeans and an ironed T-shirt, but he struck Joe as not being very relaxed or casual. Maybe it was the carefully combed and parted dark brown hair, or the evenly tanned face, Frank thought. His casual look seemed organized and affected.

"Hey, look who I ran into," Rob said excitedly. "Frank and Joe Hardy, this is Jeremy Foote, the account executive I told you about," he said. Frank and Joe shook hands with the ad man, who gave them a wide smile. "Good to meet you both," he said in a smooth, deep voice. "Rob's been telling me about his newest o-ing recruits."

Frank smiled. "I think we still have a lot to learn."

57

Jeremy clapped Rob on the back. "Well, Rob's the man to teach you," he said. "Speaking of that, Mr. O-ing," he said to Rob with a smile, "we need to get this photo shoot set up. I've got to get back home."

"I thought you might be staying for a while," Rob said. "Dad said you came out a few days ago."

"Oh. Well, to tell you the truth," Jeremy said in a confidential tone, "Andy, my photographer, and I decided to slip in a little camping. I don't think your dad will mind, but do me a favor, Rob. Don't tell him, okay? I don't want him to get the idea that I'm slacking off."

Rob shook his head. "You know Dad doesn't think that," he said.

"Sure, sure," Jeremy said with a weary grin. "Anyway, we're here now. I'll call you at the hotel so we can set up the photo shoot." Jeremy shook hands with Rob and the Hardys again before he left.

"That was a surprise," Rob said when Jeremy had gone. "But it's good to see Jeremy again. Did you find out anything about the visor?"

Joe told Rob what the store manager had said, then added, "I think we should get going."

Rob nodded, and a few moments later Joe and the others were enjoying the beautiful ride to the Middle Fork.

Twenty miles north of Stanley they saw the river. Its level seemed very high to Joe, probably due to the winter snows and spring rains, he guessed.

On the trip up, Sylvia had the group howling with laughter over stories of Rob's and her many misadventures on the o-ing trail. Joe realized that Sylvia could be a lot of fun when she wasn't being jealous. He started to understand what Rob saw in the girl and wondered if someone as clever as Sylvia would ever really stoop to threaten an old boyfriend.

Rob pulled into the parking lot of an old-fashioned log lodge built to overlook the river.

The group piled out of the car and filed into an outdoor eating area, where thick rough-hewn tables were scattered about a patio. Pine trees surrounded the patio, and from below the sooth-ing sound of the river could be heard.

"Mmmm, this looks great," Sylvia said, open-ing a menu and reading. "I say we get one of everything and pass it around to share."

"What they ought to do is hand out fishing poles instead of menus," Frank said to her. "That way we could have lunch and entertain-ment, too."

Joe chuckled and put his menu down on the table, figuring he'd just have a burger and fries. He idly gazed at the other people on the patio, trying to see what they were eating. Finally his gaze rested on two men and a woman sitting at a small square table a few yards away. The woman, in her early thirties, was small and dark skinned, with a long braid down her back. She sat facing Joe, and beside her sat a young man about Rob's age with shoulder-length blond hair. Facing the two, with his back to Joe's table, was a young man with straight, dark hair.

Joe sat bolt upright in his chair.

"Hey, Rob," he said, his voice low, "isn't that Takashi Okira over there?"

Rob had to swivel his head to peer over his shoulder at the table. He stared intently, then whirled back around to face his friends.

"It's Takashi, all right," Rob said, his voice demonstrating his shock. "And worse, he's eating lunch with the enemy!"

Chapter

7

"I CAN'T BELIEVE IT," Sylvia said quietly. "Isn't that the Northern Cal coach?"

"Sure is," Rob muttered.

"What are you talking about?" Joe asked.

"That's Malika Morris," Rob explained. "She's the coach of Northern California State University's orienteering team."

"Idaho State's biggest rival," Sylvia put in.

"Northern Cal came in second at the nationals last year," Rob said, his voice low. "In fact, they come in second at almost every meet. At last year's nationals Malika Morris swore she'd get the title this year—no matter what."

"Face it, Rob," Sylvia said. "You're the reason Idaho State won. You're the one she *really* wants to beat."

"Who's the blond guy?" Joe asked, eyeing the sleepy-looking young man beside Takashi.

"That's Terence Zane. He's on the Northern Cal team," Rob said. "He's pretty good—though I heard a rumor recently that he fouled one of his own teammates on a course. But what I really want to know is what Takashi's doing with them," Rob said suspiciously. "He shouldn't even be looking at those two until after the nationals."

Joe shook his head. "There's something about them—" All at once he snapped his fingers. "That's it!" He turned to Frank. "Remember yesterday, when you fell into that crevice and I had to yell for help? I'm pretty sure those were the two people who ran away."

"Malika and Terence?" Rob said in disbelief.

Joe nodded. "I only saw them from a distance, but I remember that braid."

Rob leaned forward, his eyes glittering. "You guys were running in a restricted area. It's off limits to all the timed participants in the Sawtooth meet, and coach told me that some Northern Cal o-ers have definitely entered!"

"You think Malika and Terence were scoping out the course?" Joe asked with interest.

"Well, if that *was* them you saw, I don't think they were out for a nature walk," Rob said bitterly. "Time for a little social call," he said as he stood up.

Rob walked the few yards across the patio to

Takashi's table. "What a coincidence," he said cheerily. "Funny how we keep running into each other."

"Yeah." Takashi lifted his head to Rob. He caught sight of Joe and Frank at the nearby table and said, "Still traveling with your entourage, I see."

"And you with yours," Rob said, indicating Malika and Terence. "I didn't realize the three of you were friends. How interesting." He nodded his head slowly.

"I expected a friendlier greeting from you, Rob," Malika said. "After all, when we win the nationals this year, you may want to ask us for some pointers," she said, grinning wickedly.

Terence laughed. "Yeah," he said.

"Still as witty as ever, huh, Terence?" Rob said. Ignoring Malika's comment, he turned to Takashi. "What are you doing here with them?" he said in a more serious tone.

"None of your business," Takashi said defensively. "I can have lunch with anybody I choose."

"Come off it, Rob," Malika said. "You're acting paranoid." She leaned toward him. "Are you all right? You look awfully stressed to me."

Joe jumped up from his chair and stepped forward angrily. "Maybe you'll change your tune after Rob wins," he said to Malika, "and after the whole country sees him in his athletic shoe ads."

"Ads?" Takashi said, leaning forward. "You're

letting your daddy run your career again? I can't believe it!''

Joe instantly realized he'd made a mistake in mentioning the ads. Suddenly Frank appeared behind them. ''The waitress wants to take our order,'' he said quietly. ''I think it's about time to end this little social visit.'' As they turned back, Malika called out, ''I hope you're practicing, Rob—hard.''

''Whew!'' Callie said a few minutes later, when Takashi, Malika, and Terence left. ''I didn't realize you guys were so intense.''

''Look, everybody, I'm sorry about that little scene,'' Rob said glumly. ''I just want to know what Takashi's up to.''

''Maybe he was just eating with them,'' Sylvia suggested.

Rob shook his head. ''Takashi being Mr. Friendly? Not this close to the nationals. And Northern Cal never comes out here. There's just something weird about it.''

Joe thought Rob was right. It was weird. It was too convenient for Takashi and Malika to be meeting at the same restaurant as Rob. Joe was sure now that Malika and Terence were the people who had run away when he'd called for help. Could they have something to do with the attacks on Rob?

As soon as the group finished eating, they boarded a bus to take them to where the rafts were launched.

Joe took a seat on the bus directly behind Sylvia and Rob, and when Rob walked up the aisle to chat with the driver, Joe saw his chance to talk to Sylvia. Before he could approach her, though, the college senior turned suddenly in her seat to face him.

"Joe, Rob told me what happened in his hotel room last night," she said, her beautiful brown eyes glistening with intensity. "Snakes are horrible—and it's so cruel to put one in the same room with him."

"When did Rob tell you this?" Joe asked.

"As we were walking to the bus," Sylvia replied. "He thinks Malika Morris might have had something to do with it. What do you think?"

"I think we have plenty of leads, but not a single piece of solid evidence. Which reminds me," he added without much confidence, "I tried to find your hotel yesterday so I could talk to you about this. Where are you staying?"

Sylvia's face reddened. "You found me out, huh? Don't tell Rob, okay? I told him I'd rented a room with my friends at a bed-and-breakfast because I thought that was what he'd like to hear. I knew he was with two girls from Bayport, and I wanted to look sophisticated compared to them. I know it was dumb, but I can't help it."

She eyed Joe guiltily, then added in a low voice, "Actually, I'm staying at a cheap motel outside of Ketchum."

In spite of himself, Joe really liked this girl, and he knew he'd lost one of his suspects.

Middle Fork Excursions was based in a small aluminum building on a calm spot in the river. After the rafters had signed in and put on their orange life jackets, they were introduced to Rich Harney, their guide. Rich, a bearded, sturdy man in his early twenties, led the group to the yellow rafts that floated at the river's edge.

As they reached the rafts, Callie bent down to feel the water. "Whoa! Not exactly warm, is it?" she said, pulling her hand back.

Rich smiled. "It's still early in the season. The river catches the snow runoff and stays pretty cold all year," he told her.

Sylvia stared skeptically at the river. "We won't have to be *in* the river, right?"

"Not if I can help it," Rich said. "You'll get wet—but you'll be inside the raft." He pointed out the craft they'd be taking. It had three places to sit on either side, and a seat in the bow for the guide. Joe and Liz scrambled for seats at the front. Rob and Sylvia sat behind them, and Frank and Callie behind them. Each of them grabbed a paddle as Rich and another guide pushed them into the river.

Soon Frank felt the current in the river begin carrying the raft along at a comfortable clip. In this calmer section Rich was able to keep the raft on course, using his oar to steer from the front. The others paddled from the right or left side when necessary. Most of the time they were able to relax and enjoy the scenery. Frank could see other rafts on the river.

After an unusually sharp turn, the river suddenly took a nosedive and picked up speed. Frank and the others started to bounce around as the raft began to buck like a wild horse. "Hang on!" Rich yelled above the roar of the water. "Follow my paddling if you can!"

The current was much swifter, and rocks stuck up from the water's surface like miniature icebergs. "Wow!" Frank heard Liz yell. Just then a clap of water hit her side of the raft, soaking her, Sylvia, and Frank with its spray. "This is wild!" she exclaimed.

Rob caught Liz's eye, and his face broke out into a grin. "It's great, isn't it?" he yelled to Liz. Frank noticed Sylvia studying her wet clothes in dismay and chuckled. Sylvia didn't seem to be having the "great" time Rob and Liz were.

The rapids quickly gave way to quieter waters. Rich turned his head to check on the others. "Everybody okay?" he said, smiling.

"A little wet," Frank called to Rich, "but ready for more."

"Wet and *cold*," Sylvia said. "This water is freezing."

"But isn't it fun?" Rob said with enthusiasm. Sylvia turned a skeptical eye on him. "Uh, yeah, I guess so," she said gamely. Callie and Frank had to suppress smiles.

In the distance Frank saw white water and jagged rocks. The entire river seemed to be funneling directly into the steep, roller-coasterlike tumble of water and stone, and Frank felt the raft speed up as it neared the first rocks. "Brace yourselves!" he shouted.

Just then Frank heard a loud *thwack*. "Oh!" Sylvia exclaimed. "What was that?"

The raft trembled beneath Frank. He peered over the side, where he found a two-inch hole ripped through the back of the raft. Frank could hear the air escaping with a great sound.

"What's wrong?" he heard Callie yell over the rising noise of the river.

"Bad news!" Frank yelled back. "I may be wrong—but I think we're sinking!"

Chapter
8

"WE'RE WHAT?" Rich Harney's head whipped around in surprise. "What's going on back there?"

"Something's punctured the raft!" Frank shouted up to the guide. "Did you see anything hit us?"

Rich shrugged. "I only thought I heard a pop."

"Great!" Sylvia cried. "What do we do now?"

"First, we stay calm," Rich ordered in a steady voice. "Start paddling to the right. We'll try to hit the shore before we reach the rapids."

Frank stared down the river at the rushing, foamy currents about a hundred yards ahead of them and dug his paddle into the water. He could feel the raft go slack beneath him and see the churning water occasionally slap over the drooping left side. In front of him, the raft alongside Sylvia and Liz had really begun to sag and sink. Though all seven passengers were paddling furiously, Frank could see they were making little headway against the strong currents.

Suddenly the raft shot down a narrow chute of water. Sylvia screamed as a churning mass of white water tore at them from every side. The raft was very low in the water. It felt as if it lost air every time the water pounded at it.

Just then the raft smashed into a half-submerged log, causing another, even bigger jolt. Frank heard a shout and saw Sylvia and Liz slip out of the raft as it began to collapse. The girls disappeared into the swirling waters.

"Sylvia!" Rob yelled, lunging toward the side. Frank saw Joe instinctively drop his oar in the raft and dive into the icy river. As he jumped, the raft tilted. In the next instant everyone tumbled into the river in a confusing flurry of water and oars.

The cold water sent shock waves through Frank. He surfaced, fighting the current and the cold. He quickly spotted Callie. She was being carried downstream by the force of the current, unable to swim against it.

As Frank tried to reach Callie, he saw Rich Harney bob up from behind the raft. Rich had managed to hold on to his oar, and now he was extending it toward Callie. She grasped the wide end of the oar, and he towed her toward the calmer waters near the shore. Frank swam in the direction Rich had taken.

In the meantime Joe had grabbed Sylvia. "Relax!" he yelled as she continued to flail about. "It'll make it easier." With one arm hooked around her, Joe tried to fight free of the current that was forcing them downstream, but Joe knew he was fighting a losing battle.

Suddenly he heard Rob yell, "Joe!" He looked over to where Rob and Liz were bobbing in a calm pocket by the left bank. Rob pointed to a big rock sticking up a few yards downstream from Joe and yelled, "Grab it!"

Giving in to the current, Joe and Sylvia shot right to the rock. "Don't miss it!" Joe yelled to Sylvia. With a final surge the current heaved them at the rock. Joe let go of Sylvia, and the two clung desperately to the slippery gray rock. Joe fought to hang on against the current as spray from the rapids rose over his head.

"Now over here!" Joe heard Rob shout. Joe twisted his head to see Rob pointing to the back of the rock. He realized that by following the current to the left of the rock, he and Sylvia could be carried toward Rob and calmer waters.

"Let's go!" he shouted, pointing at the other side of the rock. Sylvia nodded.

The two inched around the boulder. When they reached the edge, Joe yelled, "Now!" The two flung themselves into the current, which tore them away from the rock. Seconds later Joe felt the water slow. He looked up to see Rob swimming out to grab an exhausted Sylvia. She clung to him, relieved.

Joe, Rob, and Sylvia joined Liz in the shallows. They all stood still a moment, breathing heavily. Across the river, Joe could see Frank, Callie, and Rich being picked up by another raft, which had also grabbed their deflated raft.

"What now?" Liz said.

"Start hitchhiking," Joe said, looking upstream for another raft.

In a few minutes a large raft made its way over to the stranded foursome. "Need some help?" the guide called out. All four shouted, "Yes!"

The raft took them back to the landing. On the shore Joe found Frank, Callie, and Rich. Rich and Frank had already spread their deflated raft on the ground to take a look at the punctures. Joe joined them.

"There are two openings," Frank said to Joe, showing him both holes.

Joe looked a little startled. "*Two* openings? So we didn't just get caught on a rock or branch," he said.

Frank shook his head, frowning, as he studied the holes. One was on the top side of the raft, the other, at an angle from the first, was on the underside.

"Check this out," Joe said, looking at the top hole. "Half of the opening is a small semicircle, then the rest of the opening looks as if it was just torn away."

"So?" said Liz, who was standing over Joe.

"So," Joe said slowly, "it looks like a bullet hole."

There was dead silence among the group. Then Rob spoke. "A bullet hole? Are you sure?" he said, his voice dry and quiet.

"It looks like these are entrance and exit holes," Frank said. "And I'll bet if we could go back to that spot on the river where we were hit and draw a line from one of those holes to the other one, it would point straight to the cliffs on the right bank of the river."

"And at that point someone took a shot at us?" Rob said.

"I don't know that *we* were shot at," Frank said cautiously. "It was the raft that was hit. Did anyone see or hear anything before the raft started sinking?" Callie, Liz, and Sylvia all shook their heads.

Finally Rich said, "I don't know what's happened here, so I think I'd better call the sheriff and ask him to take a look."

As Rich walked away, Rob blurted out, "What are we playing this game for? We all know that I was the cause of this. Somebody's trying to get rid of me." He kicked the deflated raft angrily. "A couple more inches, Frank, and that hole would have been in you."

"But it wasn't," Callie said firmly. "Everyone's all right, and that's what's important."

Rob shook his head. "Anyone who's around me is in danger."

"Well, what do you expect, Rob?" Sylvia cut in, her voice edged with anger. "You and the other o-ers are so obsessed with competing that it doesn't surprise me that one of you finally flipped out." She closed her mouth abruptly, then tossed her head in disgust. "I'm freezing. I think I'll wait for the sheriff in the car."

Rob sighed as Sylvia stalked off down the trail. "She's probably right," he said, getting to his feet and starting down the trail behind Sylvia.

Joe turned to Frank. "At least we know for sure now that Sylvia has nothing to do with this," he said. "She was in as much danger as the rest of us when the raft was shot at."

Frank nodded. "It's nice to have proof she didn't do it," he said wryly. "But how do we find out who did it?"

The interviews with the sheriff took another hour. By that time, the sheriff explained, the chances of finding the shooter were close to zero. "We'll check the trail for tracks, but we get heavy traffic from hikers this time of year. The thing I can't figure is why anybody would shoot at a raft. You kids know any reason why?''

The group answered with silence. Finally the sheriff sighed and asked the rafters not to leave the Sun Valley area without letting him know. Joe and the others trooped off with Rob to return to their hotel.

The trip back was tense and silent. Joe and Frank wanted to talk about the shooting, but Rob acted as if he'd shoot anyone who opened his mouth. Callie and the girls tried to make small talk but quickly gave up.

It was late afternoon by the time Joe and Frank reached their hotel room. The minute he closed the door behind them, Joe asked Frank, "So who do *you* think took that shot?" He kicked off his wet sneakers.

"I know three people who were at Middle Fork today—and knew where we were," Frank replied.

"Takashi, Malika Morris, and Terence Zane," Joe said, nodding as if he'd been thinking the same thing. "And it's obvious they really want to play with Rob's mind before the nationals. What do you think about the fact that Takashi was having lunch with the rival team's coach?"

"I think it was more than just a casual get-together," Frank said, removing his damp T-shirt.

"Do you think they've teamed up to get Rob?" Joe asked.

"Maybe," Frank said, shrugging. "Assuming they had access to a typewriter, they could have sent Rob those notes."

"So you think the shooting is connected to the notes Rob got?" Joe asked his brother.

"If they're not," Frank said, "then Rob has two different people gunning for him—literally. That's more attention than anyone wants."

Joe shook his head. "Rob just doesn't seem like the kind of guy who'd make one enemy, much less two."

"Keep thinking about it," Frank said, heading for the bathroom. "I'm going to shower. I told Liz and Callie we'd meet them for dinner."

Joe nodded, lost in thought. As Frank closed the door to the bathroom, Joe put on some dry sneakers and grabbed his wallet and the room key. If Takashi wrote the notes, he'd have to have access to a typewriter. A quick visit to Takashi's room should answer that question. Joe kicked himself for not noticing the last time he'd been there.

Letting himself out into the hallway, Joe walked swiftly to Takashi's room. He gave three hard knocks on the door and waited. There was no answer.

Reaching into his wallet, Joe pulled out a credit card. Sliding it between the door and door frame, he glanced quickly up and down the hall. No one in sight. Joe wriggled the card into the space between the latch and the door frame. Another wriggle and the lock clicked.

Slowly he pushed open the door. After taking a quick peek down the hall, he stepped into the room, leaving the door slightly ajar.

As his eyes adjusted to the darkness, Joe studied the room. A long dresser sat just in front of him, and a double bed stood to the left of the dresser.

Joe heard a faint creaking to his left. "Who's there?" he cried.

There was no answer, only a crushing blow to the back of Joe's head. He tried to yell as the world went black and he sank slowly to his knees.

Chapter

9

JOE BLINKED RAPIDLY, trying to recover his balance as the room continued to spin around him. He was down on his knees now, and somewhere in the dark room he knew someone was waiting to strike him again.

Joe tried to raise his arms to ward off the expected blow, but his arms wouldn't obey. As his head started to clear, he heard a sound ahead of him. Finally he sprang up and threw a punch out in front of him. He felt his fist land solidly in his assailant's abdomen and heard a surprised "Oof!"

"Gotcha!" Joe said. By the dim light filtering in from the hall, Joe made out the silhouette of Takashi Okira.

"Not quite," Takashi blurted out, throwing a punch of his own. Joe blocked it with a forearm and threw another right-hand punch to Takashi's stomach. Takashi's breath whooshed out, but he still managed to throw a right jab that connected with Joe's jaw. Joe's teeth clicked together, and his head jerked back.

As Takashi danced back, his fists up, he said, "You've got a real problem, you know that?"

"Yeah," Joe retorted, shaking his head to clear it. "You." He swung out at Takashi again but was stopped by someone grabbing his arm from behind. "Wha—" he began and spun around to see Frank holding his arm.

"What are you doing?" Joe yelled.

"Trying to keep you two from killing each other," Frank said. "Looks as if I got here just in time."

"Yeah—just in time to save this weasel's hide," Takashi said angrily.

"Me?" Joe retorted, trying to pry loose from Frank. "Listen, you can quit with the attitude—we're onto your game," Joe spit out.

"The only thing you're going to be on is a police report," Takashi lashed back. "What is this now—your *second* break-in?"

"As long as you're counting, maybe you can tell me how many notes you've left for Rob," Joe shot back. He made another lunge for Takashi, but Frank held him firmly and dragged him out into the hallway. Once he cleared the doorway, Joe saw Takashi slam his door shut. He glared at the door for a moment, then sighed, relaxing his muscles. "You can let go now," he said to Frank.

Frank slowly released his brother. "What was that all about?" he asked Joe.

"I was ambushed," Joe said. "I knocked on his door, and when there was no answer, I just let myself in," he said, shrugging. "I thought you were taking a shower," he said to Frank.

"I needed to get my shampoo from my suitcase," Frank said. "And when I didn't see you in the room, I had a feeling you might be here."

"I think Takashi's the one who's been attacking Rob and leaving the notes," Joe said. "He's competitive—and violent—enough to do almost anything."

Frank frowned. "I don't know," he said slowly. "I still think we need to find out more about Malika Morris."

"What about Malika?" a voice asked. Frank turned to see Rob and Coach Santina striding down the hallway.

"We heard you talking about Malika," Rob said. "You don't think she and Terence Zane are responsible for the shooting, do you?"

Frank put his finger to his lips and pointed to Takashi's door. The others nodded and silently followed Frank to Rob's room. As soon as Coach Santina closed the door, Frank said to Rob, "All I know is, it was a pretty strange coincidence that they just happened to be having lunch at the same place where we were rafting. What's Malika's story, anyway?"

Coach Santina answered. "The most reliable one is that she has to come up with a national title this year or Northern Cal will end her contract. The school hasn't taken kindly to playing second fiddle to ISU."

"And the way everyone sees it, if Rob weren't o-ing for Idaho State," Frank said carefully, "Malika's team would have a much better chance at taking the nationals. And Takashi would be a shoo-in for the individual title."

"You don't think Takashi's in cahoots with them, do you?" Coach Santina asked. "That boy gets crazy sometimes, I'll admit—but you can't make me believe he'd betray his own team."

Frank held up his hands. "We don't have any proof yet," he said. "But you have to admit, Coach—it looks bad. Malika and Takashi were having lunch together, and they could both benefit from Rob's absence."

Rob suddenly stood up. "I can't believe what I'm hearing," he said. "I'm being followed? People are trying to hunt me down?" He shook his head. "I'm not used to this."

Frank could see that the strain of the last few days was taking its toll on Rob. If a sniper's gun didn't put Rob out of the nationals, Frank realized, the stress of the past couple of days could easily cause him to blow the race. On the other hand, Rob needed to know what danger surrounded him.

"Somebody *has* targeted you," Frank pointed out. "Our goal now is to find him or her."

Coach Santina headed for the phone. "I'm calling the police. From now until the nationals are over, Rob's not going anywhere without a bodyguard."

"Wait, Coach." Rob reached out to stop him before he could dial the phone. "I'd rather—I know you're just trying to protect me and all, but if my dad found out what's going on, he'd have to—"

"Your father has nothing to do with this." Coach Santina picked up the receiver. "We're in an emergency situation, and as your coach I'm responsible for your welfare. And frankly, Rob, if something happened to you, I would never forgive myself."

"But Dad wants—" Rob stammered, turning red. "See, there's this ad campaign."

The Hardys watched as Coach Santina turned to Rob. Silently he hung up the phone. "What campaign?" he said. "I hadn't heard about this."

Rob explained that he'd be doing a testimonial for the Freedom line of trail-running shoes for his father's advertising agency. "I was going to tell you about it later, Coach," Rob said. "But these are only preliminary shots."

"Are you sure this is a good idea?" the coach

said, folding his arms. "You need to concentrate on preparing for the nationals in two weeks."

Rob nodded. "The photo shoot is only going to take a few hours. The point is, it could mean an incredible amount of publicity for the sport of orienteering in general, and for the ISU team in particular. I really think it would be a mistake to pass it up."

"What does that have to do with calling the police?" Santina demanded.

"It's the nature of the business," Rob said with a shrug. "Advertisers don't want anyone involved in anything questionable selling their products. Even though I'm the victim here, my dad couldn't use me on the campaign if this came out."

The lean, angular coach mulled over Rob's argument for a moment. "I still don't want to take any risks," he began.

"You won't have to, Coach. That's the great part," Rob said with his reassuring grin. "These guys here—Frank and Joe Hardy—happen to be trained, experienced detectives with plenty of experience as bodyguards. They can work on this case and watch out for attackers at the same time."

"Is that true?" Santina asked Joe, looking surprised.

"Yes, sir," Joe told him. "In fact, when I talked to you in the lobby that time, I was actually trying to dig up background information on

Takashi. He's been one of our suspects from the start.''

Coach Santina frowned. He clearly had a hard time imagining his second-best o-er as a criminal.

"Are you boys really good?" the coach asked doubtfully. The Hardys nodded, and the coach pondered for a moment. "When are these pictures being taken of you?" he asked Rob.

"Tomorrow afternoon," Rob told him. "I just talked to our account executive. Before that I'm doing another practice run in the mountains that should take most of the morning."

"Hmm." The coach frowned. "Well, make sure you take these boys along."

Joe exchanged a pleased look with Rob as the coach said good night and headed for the door.

"You're sure you don't want the police called in?" Frank asked Rob once Coach Santina was gone.

"I couldn't stand to have strangers following me around," Rob answered quickly. "At least I know you guys." His face broke into a grin. "Now—let's go eat, okay? Liz was starving last time I saw her. I bet she'll call the cops herself if we don't feed her something fast."

The next morning Joe stood at the base of a mountain inside the Sawtooth National Recreation Area, shivering. "Let's get going," he said, zipping up his sweatshirt. "I need to get my blood moving."

Joe, Frank, and Rob had just made the drive to the Sawtooth National Forest to run another practice course. Pine and fir trees covered the landscape, dipping up and down the mountains all around them. The quiet of the early morning was interrupted only by the shrill calls of blue jays and the singing of other birds.

"Don't you love this air?" Rob said, expanding his chest and drawing in a few deep breaths. "It's so pure."

"It's pure, all right," Joe said, shoving his hands in his pockets. "Pure cold."

Frank grinned. He knew Joe was envying Callie and Liz, both still asleep tucked into warm, soft beds. The girls had announced at dinner the night before that they planned to go mountain biking. Sylvia had reportedly agreed to go with the girls, and Joe had wanted to join them, also. But Frank knew that Joe would never desert Rob while he needed him—even if the fears of the night seemed ridiculous in the calm of a beautiful mountain morning.

"You guys have your maps," Rob said. "This is a short course, but it looks as if they've tried to pack in as many twists and turns and natural barriers as possible." He checked the stopclock on his wristwatch. "I'm going to time myself," he said. "I need to get in a good run."

"In other words, we'll meet you at the finish," Joe said with a frown.

Rob grinned. "I just hope I get there first."

He hit the timer button on his watch and, clutching his map and compass, took off up the mountain.

Frank handed Joe their compass while he studied the topographical map.

"I know we have zero chance of beating Rob," Joe said, squinting over his brother's shoulder at the symbols on the map. "But this time let's try not to embarrass ourselves, okay?"

"The main thing is to stick as close to him as we can," Frank reminded Joe. "We're not here to play around. We're here to watch over him."

The two agreed on their route and began jogging up the side of the mountain through the trees. The ground was still damp with morning dew as they made it to their first checkpoint. A small orange flag was stuck at the top of a ridge, and Joe punched their scorecard. "Not bad," he said, checking the compass again. "I think we're getting the hang of this."

"Not so fast," Frank cautioned as he studied the map. "That first one was easy. Now we have to go straight downhill—and there are a bunch of symbols I don't know here." He showed Joe the map. "I think as long as we stay to the right we'll be okay."

"Do you hear Rob anywhere ahead of us?" Joe asked.

Frank listened. "No. That means we need to move faster."

They began their descent, loping quickly but

carefully over slippery pine needles as they tried to maintain their footing. Joe, in the lead, decided to veer to the left to avoid a large clump of trees. Working his way around the pines, he could make out the sound of a creek below.

As the sound of rushing water became louder, Joe picked up his pace a bit. Traversing down the slope of the mountain, he flew around a bend—and pulled up short with a shout.

"Whoa!" Frank had come running around the same bend and smacked directly into Joe. Joe stumbled and fell against the huge rock formation looming above them. The Hardys had missed running into it by inches.

"Well," Frank said, putting his hand on the massive gray rock, "how'd this get here?"

He consulted the map again. "There's nothing here to indicate a giant mound of rock," he announced. "What a stupid mistake. We could have broken our noses."

"Are you kidding? We could have given ourselves concussions," Joe replied, reaching for the map. "Let me see that. How do you even know we are where we think we are?"

Just as Frank opened his mouth to reply, the Hardys heard a sharp crack nearby.

"What's that?" Joe demanded.

"I know what it was," he said urgently. "It was a gunshot."

Joe nodded. Then, rising above the echo, he heard a human cry.

Chapter

10

"THAT SOUNDED as if it came from that way,"
Joe said, starting off in the direction he was
pointing.

Frank nodded, checking the map. "Don't drift
too far toward the sound of that rushing water,"
he called after Joe. "The brush seems to get
thicker down there."

Clutching the map, Frank ran after Joe. "Watch
out ahead!" Joe yelled, suddenly veering to his
left. Frank, right behind Joe, copied his brother's move and saw that Joe's quick reflexes had
saved them from falling over a small cliff.

Just then they heard a voice calling Frank's
name. Rob was standing partially hidden by a
large tree. Frank and Joe scrambled over to him.

"Are you all right?" Joe asked, his breath coming in short gasps.

Rob nodded. "A shot came from somewhere nearby. It sounded as if it came from down by that river that's drawn on our maps," he said in a weak voice. "I think the bullet hit one of these trees. I could feel it as it flew by my head," he finished, his voice barely a whisper now.

The three stood in silence for a moment. "Could the shooter be a hunter?" Joe asked quietly.

Rob shook his head. "I doubt it. There's nothing being hunted now. Nothing's in season. Unless the shooter's a poacher. They don't obey any laws."

Frank had already begun searching the trees for the cartridge. "Stay down low and keep your eyes open," he said. "The shooter could still be around."

Frank looked back at the tree Rob had been using for cover. Moving closer, he carefully ran his eyes over the brown bark.

"Look what I found," he said to Joe and Rob as he began to chip at the bark. There, imbedded into the bark, was a small piece of metal.

"What is it?" Rob said, squinting.

"The bullet," Joe answered, pressing his own face near the tree trunk. "Good eye, Frank."

Frank had taken out his Swiss army knife and was digging the bullet out. "It's not lodged in

89

too deeply," he said, and in a matter of seconds he had pulled it from the tree.

Bending over Frank's outstretched palm, Joe took a good look at the bullet. "It was shot from a rifle," he murmured. "Maybe the same rifle that was used to hit our raft."

"But who?" Rob said. Anger had replaced fear in his voice. "That bullet could have been lodged in my head this time! I'm tired of being a target."

"You're right. This hardly seems like an accident," Frank admitted. "At least we can check out the bullet this time."

"Let's try the Sun Valley Sportcenter," Joe suggested. "They have a good-size hunting department."

"Well, there goes another orienteering run," Rob said, dejected. "For some reason, I'm not really in the mood to run through the forest, anyway."

After a short jog back to the head of the trail, the trio climbed into Rob's four-wheel drive to head to the sporting goods store. They passed a ranger station, and Frank asked Rob to pull over.

As Rob rolled down his window, a young man in khaki pants and shirt strolled over to the car. "Morning," he said. "Can I help you?"

Frank leaned over from the passenger seat. "We were just up on one of the orienteering courses," he said to the ranger. "Somebody was shooting a rifle up there. Do you know if there's anything legal to hunt at this time of year?''

The ranger seemed surprised. ''That whole area is off limits to hunters, anyway. You didn't get a look at the hunter, did you?''

Frank shook his head. ''We just heard the shot.'' He thanked the ranger again, and Rob pulled the car back onto the road.

Joe, who had been silent during the exchange with the forest ranger, suddenly spoke up. ''By the way, did anyone happen to see Takashi this morning before we left?''

Frank turned back to Joe as Rob shot him a glance in the rearview mirror. Rob started to say something but stopped, sighing in frustration instead. Frank knew that Rob didn't want to believe Takashi might be involved—but it was becoming hard not to believe it.

''We don't have any proof that Takashi is responsible for any of this,'' Frank pointed out. ''We don't know who that sun visor belonged to, or who typed the notes, or who might be calling sporting goods stores. And we don't know whose bullet this is.''

''You're right,'' Joe admitted. ''But other than Takashi or Malika, who do you think would be after Rob?''

Frank sighed. ''I don't know,'' he said. ''I just don't want to jump to any conclusions.'' They continued the ride in silence, making only one stop to pick up some sandwiches to eat in the car.

Rob pulled onto a smaller road almost back to Sun Valley. "Jeremy said the photo shoot would be here," Rob said. "There are a lot of mountain biking trails around, so who knows? We might run into the girls this afternoon."

"Aren't we early for the shoot?" Joe asked, checking out the hills around them. The taller ones were covered with large trees, while some of the others only had scrub oaks and pines.

Rob nodded. "Yeah. We are a little early. But Jeremy and Andy, his assistant, are here already. They planned to take some establishing shots this morning to show the people back home. Actually, they wanted to shoot my photos this morning, too, when the light's best—but I insisted on spending the morning working out."

Frank glanced at Rob as the athlete turned onto an even narrower dirt road. Considering that he'd just been shot at, Rob was holding up remarkably well, Frank decided. Still, everyone had his limit. It was probably a good thing that he was taking time out to work on the ad campaign. Maybe Rob—and the Hardys—could relax a little in the more businesslike atmosphere of advertising.

Rob drove until he spotted Jeremy sitting on a small metal trunk in a clearing to the right of the road. Rob pulled over, and he and the Hardys jumped out. Frank noticed as he shook hands with Jeremy that the rather short, slim account executive was still remarkably tidy and professional, even in the middle of the woods. Jeremy also seemed a little preoccupied. He was sweating, and his mouth was set in a tight line.

"You're early," he said to Rob, almost disapprovingly. "Andy is out picking some picturesque spots."

"We had to quit the workout early," Rob explained. Frank saw how hard the athlete was trying to sound casual. "I had a pain in my leg. It's gone now, though." He laughed. "Coach Santina would have said it was a case of 'slacker's knee.'"

Jeremy nodded, his mind obviously on other things. "Well, we have some great nature shots for the clients to admire," he told Rob. "If we can get a good set of prints of you in action, I think we'll have ourselves a deal. I guess this is a big day for you, huh, Rob—I mean, since your dad wants to put you on this account when you join the firm."

"I can't wait," Rob said eagerly. "Actually, I have a few ideas about trail-running shoe designs myself that I'd like to discuss with the client."

"First things first, kid," Jeremy said with a chuckle. "Good—here's Andy now."

Frank spotted a man with several cameras swinging from his neck walking toward them. "By the way, we have a new warmup suit—and new shoes, of course—for you to wear for the photos," Jeremy told Rob. "They're in the van. You might as well go ahead and change."

Rob nodded self-consciously and followed the account executive toward his van parked down the road. Frank and Joe sat in the clearing, enjoying the peace and quiet. A moment later, though, the quiet was broken as a car pulled off the road behind them.

"Who's that?" Frank asked when he saw the small sports car come to a stop behind Rob's car. His jaw dropped when he saw Malika Morris get out of the car.

Rob had apparently seen her at the same time. Frank saw the surprise on his face even from down the road. As Malika approached the clearing, Rob charged back to the clearing to challenge her.

"What are you doing here?" he demanded as the woman strode up to the Hardys.

"I happened to be in the neighborhood," Malika said sarcastically, "so I thought I'd stop by."

"How did you know where we were?" Joe asked her.

"I ran into your girlfriends at breakfast this morning," she told him. "They were very busy announcing your plans to the world."

" 'Announcing'?" Frank said skeptically. "Callie or Liz. wouldn't 'announce' anything. You must have eavesdropped on them."

"They were so loud it was hard not to overhear," Malika informed him. "At any rate, I'm glad I found out about this. It's important that we o-ers behave ethically on photo shoots like this. I hope you don't expect to make endorsement money as a college athlete, Rob," she said pointedly.

Rob rolled his eyes. "I'm not getting paid for this," he said in a tired voice. "And besides, I'll have graduated by the time the ads come out."

"Hey, Rob," Jeremy called from the van. "Come put this stuff on so we can get started." Rob walked back to the van, climbed inside, and emerged a few moments later in a lightweight blue and green warmup suit and neon blue and white shoes. Frank noted appreciatively that the trail-running shoes were a newer, sleeker version of the flat, spiked shoes Rob usually wore.

As Jeremy adjusted Rob's clothes, Joe turned to Malika. "You know, we really could use a little privacy here. Is there any chance we could get you to leave?"

"Not a chance in a million," Malika answered flatly. "This is public parkland. I have as much right to be here as you do."

"What about your o-ing team?" Frank asked with a frown. "If you want to win so badly, shouldn't you be working with your runners?"

"Mind your own business," Malika snapped at him. "Who are you two, anyway?"

"Friends of Rob's," Joe answered for his brother. "And as Rob's friends, we want to make sure he doesn't get hurt before the game. Or threatened, or victimized by some competitor who thinks it's fun.''

Malika snorted derisively. "Psych jobs are part of the game.''

"Not psych jobs that involve rattlesnakes under people's pillows. And threatening notes. And rock slides. And bullets," Joe retorted. "Where were you this morning, anyway?" he added. "Or was that your sidekick, Terence, we ran into this morning?"

"I don't have to listen to this." Malika's face reddened.

"Isn't that why you came here?" Joe insisted. "To make Rob nervous during the shoot? Maybe you think if you harass him long enough, you can blow his concentration for the nationals."

Malika turned away abruptly as Rob approached the group.

"Frank and Joe Hardy, this is Andy Sorenson, the photographer," Rob announced. He pointedly ignored Malika as she moved away.

The Hardys shook hands with Andy, a middle-aged man with pale blond hair pulled back into a ponytail. Andy turned back to Rob. "I'd like to start with some shots of you running," he said. "Let's climb this hill a bit, and I'll shoot you going up and down it."

"Hmm. That sounds sort of familiar." Rob gave a sheepish smile to Frank and Joe as they followed Andy up the hill. Frank couldn't help but notice that Rob acted a little stiff in the new outfit.

For the next half hour Frank and Joe watched Rob run through trees, over rocks, and straight downhill, clutching a map and wearing a compass on his wrist. On his face was a look of intense—and fake—concentration. At one point Andy ordered him to run back and forth across the top of the hill, claiming that the light and shadows were just right in that spot.

"Okay," Andy called after snapping a couple of rolls. "Now I'd like some specific poses. Jeremy and I have a few locations picked out." He led Rob over to a gorge that cut between two hills. Frank, Joe, and Jeremy followed, with Malika trailing stubbornly behind.

Frank saw that far below ran a river. An old-fashioned rope-and-board bridge was suspended between the two hills over the river. Frank followed Joe to the bridge, checking out the design with interest.

"I've never seen one of these, except in the movies," Frank said to his brother.

Joe, peering forty feet down to the creek, shook his head appreciatively. "It'll make a good backdrop for a photo," he remarked.

The two moved out of the way as Rob was positioned in front of the bridge. Andy bobbed back and forth, trying to get the best angle. Finally he settled himself at a point a little below Rob's level on the side of the hill. "Ready to

97

move across," he called out to Rob. "Remember, go slowly, but make it look as if you're going fast," he instructed.

Rob looked at Frank and Joe skeptically. Joe grinned. "Let's see if he can do a slow-motion expression," he said to Frank. He noticed that Malika had moved up to watch this series of shots.

Grasping the rope sides of the bridge, Rob began walking across the old boards. The bridge sagged and swayed a bit with Rob's weight, and he had to pause to get his balance. When he began again, it was with longer strides. Joe could hear the ropes and boards creak as Rob stepped forward.

Without warning the ropes let out one loud groan and jerked violently. Rob fell to his knees, still grasping the ropes. There were a series of pops as one rope after the other snapped.

"Watch out!" Joe yelled, leaping to the edge of the gorge. To his horror, the bridge plunged into the abyss, carrying Rob down with it.

Chapter

11

"HANG ON, ROB!" Frank yelled as he and Joe raced toward the chasm's edge. Peering down, they saw a swirl of arms, legs, and rope caught in a rush of water.

"Come on, Joe!" Frank yelled. He half-ran, half-slid down the steep slope, skidding to the water's edge. Joe was right behind him.

As they reached the riverbank, Frank saw that Rob was struggling to get his face above the water. Frank tensed for one long moment as the athlete disappeared from view.

"He's lost his grip on the ropes!" Frank shouted as he watched Rob struggle to stay afloat. Frank turned to see Joe wading into the water.

He swam out to the center of the river. Grabbing a half-submerged tree root for balance, he held out his other arm to Rob.

After a few tense seconds Rob began to move toward Joe, alternately swimming and floating. Finally he grasped Joe's hand, and Joe swam with him to shore. There Frank helped lift Rob out of the water.

"Are you okay?" Frank asked.

"My knee's a little banged up—and my shin hurts," Rob admitted, still breathing hard. "I must have hit the bottom of the river. . . ."

Rob's voice trailed off, and Frank realized that he must be gritting his teeth, trying to minimize the pain. Frank realized that the o-er had finally reached his physical and mental limit.

From the top of the slope Frank heard a shout. He saw Jeremy and Andy at the edge of the gorge.

"Is he all right?" Jeremy called down to them.

"I'm fine, Jeremy," Rob said, though a painful expression remained on his face.

"Rob, I don't know what happened," Andy called down. "I checked the rope bridge myself yesterday. I'm sorry, man!"

"It's okay," Rob said weakly. "It's not your fault. Or anybody's, I guess."

Frank wasn't convinced of that. Looking past Jeremy and Andy, he spotted a third figure watching from a short distance away. It was

Malika Morris. Her eyes were wide, and she remained still, just staring down at them.

That's odd, Frank thought. You'd think she'd at least ask whether Rob was all right. "Joe," he said after a second's pause, "help Rob up the slope. I'm going to check out the bridge."

Joe nodded. "Come on, Rob. We'll take it slow."

As the two made their way up the slope, Frank swam out to where half the bridge still lay bobbing in the water. The ropes seemed to be fairly new, Frank thought. He ran his hands over them, pulling more and more of the bridge out of the water. Suddenly he stopped. A section of one of the main support ropes had been cut almost completely through.

This was no accident, Frank realized. The cut was too neat. Nowhere else was the rope frayed or torn. Frank dragged the rope bridge to shore and left it at the water's edge while he scrambled back up the slope, where he came upon the others huddled around Rob.

"Guys," Frank told them, "that bridge was sabotaged. Someone cut one of the main supports."

Everyone turned to Frank.

"Are you sure?" Rob asked, his voice quivering.

"Positive," Frank told him. "The cut was very neat and very well placed."

"I can't understand it," Andy repeated. "Jeremy, we went over this site yesterday, didn't we?''

Jeremy nodded. "It checked out fine."

While all eyes were focused on Frank, he noticed that Malika Morris was slowly sneaking away from the circle of people.

"Going somewhere, Ms. Morris?" Frank asked curtly.

Malika stopped and turned back to Frank. "Why shouldn't I?" she asked. "Certainly you don't think I had anything to do with this." When no one answered, Malika strode off to her car.

Rob sighed. "I guess we don't have any proof she did," he said dejectedly.

"I know," Frank responded, "but she *was* acting suspicious. Why would she want to spend her day watching you pose, anyway? I'm going to follow her back to her car."

"Who knows," Joe answered for him. "Maybe she thought she could ruin your focus, Rob. The main thing right now, though, is that you're okay."

The noise of spinning tires made Frank run faster. He got back in time to see Malika's car peeling out onto the dirt service road. He also saw a second car pull onto the road from the opposite shoulder and speed off after it.

"Hey," Frank said out loud. "I think that was Terence and Takashi in that car."

He ran back to tell the others. "So," Joe said. "They showed up after all."

"I didn't see them during the shoot," Rob put in. "What do you think they were up to?"

Frank and Joe shrugged. "Shoot's over for now, fellas," Jeremy said wearily. "Rob, thanks for coming. I'm really sorry about all this, and I'm glad you're okay. We'll line up another shoot tomorrow, after the Sawtooth race—if it's okay with you to work on Sunday."

"No problem, Jeremy," Rob responded. "I appreciate your concern. Please don't mention any of this to my dad, okay? I don't want him to worry."

Jeremy smiled wanly. "Fine. I just hope you feel better once you've changed. Andy and I will alert the ranger station about the bridge." Jeremy waved absently and walked off to where the photographer was packing up his equipment.

As soon as Rob had changed into his own clothes, he and the Hardys climbed back into his car. "Where to now?" Rob asked a little while later on the road into Sun Valley.

"We still need to stop by a sporting goods store to check out the bullet," Joe reminded them.

"Good idea," Frank agreed. "Let's do it."

"Can I help you boys with something?" asked the middle-aged salesman behind the counter in the Sun Valley Sportcenter's hunting and fishing section.

"I hope so," Frank began. "We were wondering if you could tell us what kind of bullet this is. I know it's a long shot—pardon the pun." Frank extended his open hand with the bullet in it. The seller took the bullet and examined it closely.

"Of course I know." The man smiled. "This is a thirty-five Whelan—a bullet we don't get much call for these days. I can tell by the copper jacket—only one bullet looks like this."

"Do you happen to remember if—" Joe started.

Before Joe could finish his question, the salesman answered it. "Actually, though, I did sell a couple of boxes of these just the other day. Wasn't a local guy—that's why I remember him."

Finally we're onto something, Joe thought. "Do you know where he was from?" he asked quickly.

"Let's see—nope, I don't think he said," the salesman said, rubbing his chin. "Must have been from some big city, though, is my guess. He wore designer-type jeans and a T-shirt without wrinkles in it. He was that type who looks as if he's in a suit even when he's not wearing one."

"Was he in his late twenties?" Joe could hear the growing excitement in Frank's voice. "Did he have dark brown hair?"

The salesman squinted, trying to remember.

"I think it was dark brown," he said at last. "He was definitely a young man. What I do remember is how much he knew about hunting. We struck up quite a conversation."

"Thanks very much, sir," Joe said, trying to suppress the excitement in his voice. He took the bullet back from the man. "Come on, guys, let's get a move on."

"We're onto something here," Joe said eagerly as the three moved quickly toward the store exit. "That was a perfect description of Jeremy Foote."

Rob shook his head angrily. "No, it wasn't. He couldn't even remember the color of the guy's hair. Besides, even if Jeremy did buy bullets, there's no way he'd use them on me. What reason would he have?"

"I know how you feel, Rob," Frank said after a moment. "And all we have is circumstantial evidence that he's the one who shot that rifle today." He took a breath and continued, "But if he did buy that bullet here . . ."

Rob glared at Frank before pushing through the store's glass door and marching off across the crowded parking lot to his car. Frank and Joe followed him.

"Let's head back to the hotel, Rob," Frank said quietly as he and Joe slipped into the car. "Callie and Liz are probably wondering where we are."

* * *

"Hi, girls," Joe called out as he entered the hotel lobby with Frank and Rob. Callie, Liz, and Sylvia were sitting on a sofa near the front desk, reading newspapers while a small group of adults in cycling clothes exchanged jokes nearby. All three girls looked tanned, relaxed, and refreshed, he noted with envy. As he approached them, he added, "Have we got some news for you."

"News?" Liz put down her newspaper as Sylvia and Rob exchanged self-conscious glances. "We've got a pretty hot tip of our own."

"What's up?" Frank asked.

"Well, after our bike ride—which by the way, Rob, was terrific—I asked the others if they'd mind coming along while I did some background research for my article at orienteering club headquarters."

"Guess what we found out?" Liz put in excitedly. "Malika signed Terence Zane up for tomorrow's race weeks ago—in person. Apparently, she was determined to put him in the competition—even though it's a small-time, open-to-the-public event."

"Maybe she wanted him in the race so he could go after Rob," Frank said thoughtfully. "It would have been an easy call to assume that the o-ing champion would use the last noncompetitive meet in the state before the nationals to warm up."

"Also, she could have gotten to know the countryside while she was here," Joe said excitedly. "At least enough to cause a certain rock slide and shoot at people on the o-ing courses."

"That was good work, Liz," Rob added with a grateful smile. "Even though it's news I don't particularly want to hear, it means a lot to me to know that you care enough to try to find out who's after me."

"Actually, it wasn't my idea to look at the registration sheet," Liz said with a grin. "It was Sylvia's. She spotted Terence's name next to Malika's signature and the date. Callie and I never even thought of playing detective."

"Wait a minute, everybody," Frank said, glancing at Rob and Joe. "This information is great, but it doesn't jibe with what we just learned. We were just going to tell you that Jeremy Foote is the one chasing Rob. Rob was shot at again today, and we think the bullet belonged to Jeremy."

"Who's Jeremy Foote?" Callie asked in the stunned silence that followed.

"He works for my father's advertising firm," Rob explained. "He's in charge of the Freedom shoe campaign. And he has nothing to do with any of this, I swear."

"He does, too!" Joe protested. Then he added weakly, "We just don't know why."

A puzzled silence descended on the crowd as they tried to piece together the day's two discoveries. Finally Frank said, "I think Joe and I should check out that orienteering club headquarters. We have to register for the meet anyway. Maybe we can pick up some rumors from the players hanging out there. Do you think it's still open, Rob?"

"There's a good chance," Rob responded, "because it's so close to the registration deadline. I'll go with you. That is," he added, checking with the girls, "if you don't mind our running off again."

"Go ahead," Sylvia said, smiling at her new friends. "We saw a couple of o-ers check in a few minutes ago. Maybe we can help Liz interview them."

"I'm sorry, guys," the race director, Kevin Nash, said, shaking his head as Rob questioned him a short time later. The Hardys and Rob had caught the tanned, light-haired man just as he was about to leave his small office, lined with enlarged maps and o-ing team photographs. Nash did allow Joe and Frank to fill in their registration forms, though, and meanwhile Rob had brought up the subject of Malika.

"I don't remember much about Ms. Morris's trip here," the director said, perching on the edge of his metal desk. "I *was* surprised to see her. Most coaches call in their squad lists on public meets, but all she did was sign up her players and leave."

"She didn't ask about the other competitors or try to find out about the course?" Rob asked.

"Nope. And there's no way she could have gotten hold of a map, Rob, if that's what you're worried about. We've really tightened our security here lately."

"Just because of the meet?" Joe asked, looking up from his writing.

"No, of course not," Nash answered with a chuckle. "We had a break-in a few days ago. Someone tried to rob the place and left it a total mess."

"Was anything taken?" Rob asked. "Like a map?"

"That's the first thing we checked, but none was missing. The burglar must have been scared off, because we didn't find anything missing. Anyway, we put locks on all our file drawers."

Frank finished writing and handed the director his registration. "Thanks for your help. I guess we'll see you tomorrow."

"You sure will." Nash winked mischievously at Rob as he took Joe's registration form as well. "The course is great. And we can always use newcomers on the slopes, can't we, Rob?"

"You bet." Rob gave the director a casual wave and headed for the door.

"Oh, wait," Nash called to Rob as the Hardys started out, too. "Take one of these compasses with you. Ms. Morris got them free as part of some promotion, and she left some with me to hand out."

Frank turned to see the director reach into a

box on his desk and take out a small plastic object. "You're welcome to them, too," Nash told the Hardys, "but Malika said they're really just for top o-ers."

"What are they?" Frank asked, moving closer to take a look.

"They're thumb compasses," Nash answered. "Coaches get freebies like this all the time from various businesses. No matter what you think about Malika personally, it *was* nice of her to leave these here."

"Let me see that," Rob said, reaching for the compass. The Hardys watched as he examined the black plastic object. It looked smaller than the one the Hardys had been using, Frank realized. He watched as Rob slipped his thumb through a leather loop that stuck out of the side. The compass now lay flat on Rob's palm.

"You're giving that compass quite a going over," Frank said. "Is it an unusual design?"

"It's a standard thumb compass," Rob said. "A lot of the top o-ers use them in races because they're easier to hang on to when you're sprinting. I have one of my own for racing," he added. "But there's something about this design—I know I've seen it before," Rob said, turning his hand around to look at the compass.

As Nash and the Hardys watched, Rob strode over to the window and looked out. Then he checked the compass. "Hey," he said, "this compass isn't pointing north."

Frank, Joe, and the director joined Rob by the window and peered at the wavering needle on the compass. "If I look straight out this window, I should be facing north," Rob told them.

"But the compass isn't registering that," Nash agreed. "That's very strange."

"It's more than strange." Rob closed his hand on the compass. "If someone used this on a course, he'd get hopelessly lost. He'd definitely lose the meet."

At that moment the door to the office opened and Malika Morris strode into the room.

"Malika?" Nash said, confused. "Maybe you could explain something for us."

Malika froze in the doorway, then abruptly turned and started to walk away.

"Wait a minute, Coach Morris!" Rob yelled, running after her into the hall. Grabbing the woman by the shoulder, he spun her around. "You're not going anywhere until you tell me why you're trying to sabotage tomorrow's meet!"

Chapter

12

"GET OUT of my way, Niles," Joe heard Malika say as he and Frank moved to the office door-way. "I didn't come here to talk to you."

"Who'd you come here to talk to, then?" Rob demanded. "Kevin Nash? Were you going to let him in on the ten best ways to booby-trap the competition?"

"Don't be ridiculous," the coach snapped. "I had some technical matters to discuss with Kevin. I'll just come back tomorrow when—"

"You left these here, hoping I'd be dumb enough to pick one up," Rob interrupted, opening his hand to reveal the compass. "And if I did take one, you hoped I wouldn't figure out that the directions were wrong until I was hopelessly lost."

Joe noticed Nash edging closer to Rob. "Um, excuse me," the director said in a low voice. "Are you sure the compass isn't just broken?"

"Sure I'm sure." Rob continued to stare at Malika, who coolly met his gaze. "You can check the box. I'll bet the compasses are all the same. Actually they're not broken. They're just from Australia."

Joe exchanged a blank look with his brother. "Australia?"

"A compass made for use in the southern hemisphere won't work up north," Rob explained curtly. "It's set for a different pole. But not many people know that. And how many people do you know who have been to Australia lately—except Malika."

Joe's eyebrows shot up. "You were in Australia?" he asked the coach.

"The World Championships were held there last year," Rob answered for her. "Coach Santina and Coach Morris both went. Coach Santina brought back the same kind of compass. That's how I recognized it."

"This is ridiculous," Malika finally said to Kevin Nash, her voice soft and trembly. "I've never seen that compass before in my life."

"But it was in the box you—" The director's voice faded as he saw the coach's expression.

"I don't know what you think gives you the right to talk to people like this," Malika growled, turning on Rob. "I guess what Takashi says is true—you're just a spoiled brat." Wrenching her shoulder from Rob's grasp, Malika turned on Nash. "I'll see you tomorrow." Then she stomped off down the hall.

"Listen, Rob," Nash said, frowning at the athlete. "If you have some kind of complaint you want to make—"

"Thanks. Maybe later," Frank said, grabbing Rob by the arm and propelling him toward the exit. "He'll let you know."

As soon as the three left the building, the Hardys began to interrogate Rob. "Are you sure about those compasses being Australian?" Joe asked urgently.

Rob nodded. "Well, I'm almost sure. I've only seen one like that once before—Coach Santina's."

Rob shook his head to clear it as they walked to his car parked in the campus lot nearby. Joe noticed that there were dark circles under his eyes, and his face was drawn and tired.

"Look, I know I sort of blew up in there," Rob said after they had climbed into the car. "But what was I supposed to think? You know Malika was hoping Nash would give one of those compasses to me."

"But we can't be sure of that," Joe said to him. "She had no way of knowing you'd take one—or even use it if you did."

"Not only that," said Frank, "she'd have to expect you not to notice that something was wrong with it. That's not very likely—as you just proved."

"But she had no way of knowing I'd seen that kind of compass before," Rob retorted.

Frank shrugged. "Joe's right. The compass alone doesn't prove that Malika's the one who's after you." He glanced at his watch. "Look, it's getting late and we're all worn out. Maybe we should just go back to the hotel. That way you can get a good night's sleep for the meet tomorrow. Joe and I'll take the girls to dinner."

Joe nodded his agreement. "Tomorrow, Frank and I will keep an eye on Malika," he assured Rob. "You just concentrate on the race."

Later that night, after the Hardys had taken Liz, Callie, and Sylvia out for pizza and said good night, Joe and Frank lay awake talking over everything that had happened. "I never guessed orienteering could be such a dangerous sport," Joe remarked, stretching out under the covers in his twin bed and gazing at the shadows on the ceiling. "What do you think Malika Morris is up to, anyway?"

Frank, in his bed near the window, sighed. "If she's up to anything, she's covering herself well. We do keep seeing her at all the wrong places at the right times, but we don't have proof that she'd hurt Rob."

Joe frowned. "One thing that's been bothering me," he admitted, "is that Malika didn't know in advance where Rob's photo shoot was being held. After they overheard Liz and Callie talking about it, they would have had to drive there pretty fast to cut the rope before we showed up."

"I know," Frank said. "And I know someone who did know where the photo shoot was going to be—Jeremy."

Joe nodded. "The same Jeremy who probably bought the kind of bullet that whizzed past Rob's head this morning."

In the darkness Joe heard Frank roll over to go to sleep. "I think we'll have our work cut out for us tomorrow," Frank said.

"I have to admit every time I drive through one of the parks in this state, I'm bowled over by its beauty," Rob said with his usual cheerful smile. It was eight the next morning, and with Rob at the wheel, the Hardys, Callie, Liz, and Sylvia were driving through the front gates of the Sawtooth National Recreation Area on their way to Rob's orienteering race.

Liz, in the backseat, gazed at the magnificent mountains that framed the park's entrance. "You're right," she said. "This place is awesome."

Squeezed between Liz and Callie, Frank tried to catch a glimpse of Rob's face in the rearview mirror. He couldn't tell if Rob was just trying on some pregame optimism, or if he really did feel more confident.

"Which way now?" Rob asked. Joe, scrunched in the front seat between Sylvia and the car door, consulted the directions in his hand.

"Take a left at the next intersection, then follow that road all the way to the end," Joe told him.

"I know this road," Rob said. "The course must be tough if it's hidden back here."

"That's good," Sylvia reminded him. "It'll be great practice for you."

The group fell silent as the car continued down the narrow drive. Frank admired the tall trees pressing close on either side until he remembered that scenery was not what he and Joe were there to watch. They had entered the race to keep a close eye on Rob.

Reaching the course area, Rob parked the car in a field near the tent that housed the meet's headquarters. Frank and Rob led the way to the tent. There, dozens of race entrants, many with numbers already pinned to their shirts or jackets, were pacing. Frank noticed that the majority were around Rob's age. The air was charged with anticipation as serious athletes mixed with first-time o-ers.

"There you are," Frank heard someone say. He turned to see Coach Santina approaching them from across the large tent. "Right on time, I'm glad to see." Santina patted Rob on the shoulder, then turned to Frank and Joe. "Ready for your first race?" he asked.

"I'm just happy we're not the only ones not wearing those neon-colored jumpsuits," Joe remarked, gazing at the assorted denim shirts, ripped pants, and worn running shoes worn by the less serious athletes. Interspersed among these were the men and women who wore shin guards and waist packs over baggy nylon suits with lightweight, ventilated gloves.

"You may wish you had them in half an hour or so," Santina told him. "Those thorns can tear you up when you're running top-speed through the woods." Moving closer, he asked Joe, "Have you and Rob had any trouble since we last talked?"

"A little," Joe admitted, trying not to worry the coach. "But we're on top of it."

"Good." Santina stepped back. "Go get your control cards," he told them. "The line's right over there."

Joe noticed that Liz had wandered off, snapping photographs of athletes, and Sylvia stood nearby talking to an o-er. "Don't go to the starting line without saying goodbye," Callie called out.

Joe gave Callie a mock salute and followed Rob and Frank to the short line that had formed in front of a folding table. When they finally got to the head of the line, the Hardys were surprised to see who was at their table.

"Jeremy," Rob said, startled. "What are you doing here?"

Jeremy shrugged good-naturedly. "I got talked into volunteering when I stopped by the club headquarters for some props to use at the photo session this afternoon. It's ridiculous, I know, since I've never played the sport. But I figured this way I'd be here to cheer you on." As he handed control cards to Rob, Frank, and Joe, a big smile appeared on Jeremy's face. "Good luck, Rob," he said. "Or do o-ers say Break a leg?"

"That's weird," Joe said as the three exited the tent. "Jeremy doesn't strike me as the volunteering type."

"Who knows what type Jeremy is?" Rob said moodily, all his spirit evaporated. "I thought I knew, but now I'm confused."

"You guys all set?" Liz asked, approaching Frank and Joe and snapping their picture.

"We have our control cards. They'll give us the maps a few minutes before we start," Rob told her.

Liz nodded. "I know. I've been getting all kinds of information from people just by walking around. It almost makes me wish I were racing—but I think I'll get more story material observing."

Just then Coach Santina rejoined the group. "Okay, boys," he said, putting an arm around the shoulders of each Hardy. "Keep one eye on

119

the map and one eye on the terrain. The course looks rough. Lots of rocks, obstacles, and potential dead ends."

Santina turned to Liz, Callie, and Sylvia. "Would you like to watch the race from one of the observation towers? They're old fire ranger stations and overlook most of this part of Sawtooth. You get a better idea of the runners' speed and strategy from there."

"Terrific," Liz answered.

"Okay. We'll head over there as soon as I talk to Takashi," the coach said, nodding toward the parking area. Joe turned to see Takashi practicing some short sprints. "Rob, boys—good luck."

"Thanks, Coach," Rob replied.

"Good luck from us, too," Liz called back as she followed Callie and the coach. "See you at the finish."

Joe noticed that Sylvia hung back a little. "Rob," she said.

When Rob looked up, Sylvia held up her hand, making an okay sign with her thumb and index finger. Then she winked and walked away.

Rob was a little embarrassed. "She gives me the okay sign for luck before every race," he explained.

Frank smiled. "Seems to have worked," he noted. Static broke through as a loudspeaker cleared. An official-sounding male voice called out, "Contestants, report to the start."

His pulse beating fast, Frank turned toward the start line a short distance away.

"See you at the finish," Rob called as Frank and Joe headed toward it.

"I hope so," Frank muttered under his breath to his brother, while waving at Rob. "Let's not forget why you and I are really in this race," he added.

"I know," Joe agreed. "Malika, Takashi, Jeremy—they're all here. Anything can happen. We may not be able to keep up with Rob, but we're going to have to stay close behind him."

"Here are your maps," a voice said as Frank and Joe arrived at the start. Frank turned to take his—and realized that the person handing them out was Jeremy.

"Thanks," Frank said. He wanted to ask Jeremy why he was working so hard, but the meet was about to start and he became distracted. Nervously Frank opened his map to see the now-familiar smattering of colored blobs overlaid with thin circular lines, thicker broken lines, and a few dotted ones. "Try to plot a course to the first checkpoint," Frank suggested when he saw Joe staring at his map with his mouth open. Two minutes later the Hardys—along with several other novices—were off.

"Hold on, Joe!" Frank called a moment later as the starting gun blasted and Frank's brother went bolting into the woods. "We should stick together, right?"

"Oh—right," Joe said, slowing down reluctantly as the other novices loped past him. "But if that's the case, you're going to have to follow me." Joe led Frank up a steep hill toward the first control point. Other o-ers darted in and out of the trees, giving Frank confidence that they weren't completely lost—yet. Less than five minutes after passing the first checkpoint, though, Joe came to an abrupt stop ahead of him. Frank saw that they had dead-ended at an impassable gorge.

"Smart move, Joe," Frank said as they backed down the hill. "You only cost us ten minutes with your stellar skills."

"Hey—" Joe was about to counter. Out of the corner of his eye, Joe saw Rob race past. "Go for it, Rob," he called out.

Rob waved quickly. Frank could see the focused intent in Rob's every move. Within a few seconds Rob was far ahead of Frank and Joe, running down a steep decline.

"Let's get moving," Joe said. "This downhill will help us make up for lost time." Joe led Frank along the path Rob had blazed. "According to the map, we can save time to the next checkpoint by running this way," Joe called over his shoulder to Frank. As Joe sped through an area with few trees to slow them down, Frank was right on his heels. Finding themselves on the edge of a ridge, the two picked up speed again as they caught the downslope of another hill. The steep decline had them hurtling almost out of control. Frank couldn't focus on the trees whizzing past as he and his brother leapt fallen logs, boulders, and bushes.

"Can this be the right way?" Frank called skeptically, gasping for breath. "I don't see any other racers. What's the map say?"

"Forget the map," Joe called, breathless and tense. "Let's just make it down the hill."

Joe was now about ten yards ahead of his older brother. To Frank, Joe seemed to be out of control. Frank picked up his pace and, reaching Joe, he threw out a hand to try to slow him down. Because of thick undergrowth the two were forced to run through a narrow opening in the trees. Still plunging at breakneck speed, Frank and Joe simultaneously hurdled a large tree root.

"Hey!" Frank yelled in midflight. From the corner of his eye, he saw something flash by. It took a half second before Frank realized it was someone running.

Then, as Frank thought he was touching solid ground, the earth gave way beneath him. Panic hit all at once, and Frank's stomach rose to his throat.

He tumbled and spun out of control as a rush of dirt and rocks cascaded down on him. Frank was falling deep into a hidden pit!

Chapter

13

"THAT PIT WASN'T shown on the map," Joe groaned as he brushed dirt out of his hair and slowly got to his feet. His head was pounding, and every muscle in his body ached in protest.

Next to him in the hole, which Joe realized now was about five feet across, Frank knelt, dusting himself off. After a few seconds he stood up next to Joe.

"Are you okay?" Frank asked.

"I'm fine," Joe answered as he stared up out of the pit. On his tiptoes he could just see over the top. "But where did this come from? I didn't know six-and-a-half-foot holes just appeared out of nowhere."

Frank shook his head, watching twigs and dirt fly off from it. "I didn't, either, and I don't like this one bit. Let's get out of here."

Joe dug his fingers into the steep side. Handfuls of soil crumbled to the floor. "These walls are too loose to scale," he said. "Give me a boost, will you?"

Frank bent down and gave Joe five fingers up. Straining under his brother's weight, Frank rose and gave a final push so Joe could spring out of the hole. The first thing Joe spied was a rope tied to a tree trunk next to the pit.

"Hey," he called down to Frank. "I'll have you out in a sec." Joe tossed the free end of the rope down to Frank. "Hold on and pull yourself up," he said.

Frank quickly scaled the wall.

"What an interesting coincidence that this rope was right here," Joe commented, raising an eyebrow. "Someone must have recently dug this hole. The dirt is moist and dark at the bottom, and this rope looks brand-new, too."

Frank nodded. "Whoever dug it needed the rope to climb back out." He pulled his course map from his pocket. "And I think I know who did it," he continued. "Just as we were jumping over that root, I saw someone out of the corner of my eye, and that someone looked a lot like Jeremy Foote."

Joe's eyes widened. "I *knew* there was something funny about his volunteer work at the start of the race,'' Joe said, slamming his fist into his palm. ''First he's buying the same type of bullets that almost hit Rob, and then he sets up a photo shoot that almost kills him. Frank, it's staring us in the face—Jeremy has to be the one who's after Rob!''

Frank nodded, chewing his lower lip thoughtfully. ''But what's his motive? Malika had reason to knock Rob out of the race. It would give her team an edge. The warning notes told Rob to get out of orienteering. It doesn't seem logical for Jeremy to attack Rob and leave notes about a sport he doesn't even know.''

''Unless—'' Joe said slowly. ''Do you remember Rob telling us that he'd be working on one of Jeremy's big accounts when he graduates from college in a couple of weeks? I wonder what Jeremy thinks about the boss's son moving in on his territory?''

Frank frowned. ''You think Jeremy would attack Rob because he's worried that Rob will take his job away? That seems extreme.''

''Yeah,'' Joe said, getting more excited. ''But Rob told us that Jeremy's been at the firm for seven years, since he graduated from college. Maybe he sees Rob as destroying all those years of hard work. He could believe Rob was threatening his entire career.''

''Jeremy does strike me as an ambitious guy,'' Frank admitted. ''Still—he'd have to be over the edge to go after Rob like that.''

Frank glanced around to make sure no one was listening. "Anyway, I know one thing—we shouldn't be worrying right now about *why* Jeremy's after Rob. The fact is, Rob could be in grave danger. If there was one trap, there could be another. We have to warn Rob."

Frank took out his o-ing map and studied it again. "The checkpoint is this way." He pointed toward a densely wooded mountain terrain to the north. "Let's go."

The Hardys took off at top speed, with Frank leading his brother on a grueling sprint up steeply graded slopes. The two brothers were silent as they ran hard.

"This way, Joe," Frank gasped between fast breaths. "This last bit should put us right at the next control point. Maybe we can figure out where Rob would be once we get there."

The Hardys redoubled their speed. At the top was a small plateau. As they paused to catch their breath, Frank spotted the familiar triangular flag marking the control point. The stake supporting the flag was wedged to one side of a large boulder standing alone on the level ground.

Frank noticed several runners racing through the forest below the plateau on their way to or from the control point. A race official wearing a T-shirt with a logo for the Sawtooth meet printed on it stood nearby, checking off entrants and their times.

"There's Malika," Joe said, pointing. Frank spotted the dark-haired coach a short distance from the race official, calling out the time as Terence Zane punched his card at the flag.

"Let's go," Frank said, loping across the plateau to the control point. When he reached the flag, he grabbed the holepunch and marked his scorecard.

"Excuse me—how long ago did Rob Niles come by?" Frank called out breathlessly to the race official.

The young, athletic-looking official and Coach Morris looked surprised.

"He hasn't come through here yet," Malika told them curtly. "And neither has Takashi."

"We expected them much earlier," the official added. "Terence just ran by."

Frank and Joe were both thinking the same thing.

"Something must have happened between the time Rob passed us and this checkpoint," Frank said in a tight voice. "Can you alert race officials that Rob may be hurt? We're going to try to find him."

"Sure," the official said hesitantly. "But—"

"What's going on?" Coach Morris said, her voice rising.

"Just do it!" Frank demanded. "We don't have time to explain. But believe me, Rob is probably in trouble." Frank and Joe took off in the direction from which they'd come.

After ten minutes of furious backtracking the Hardys arrived back near the pit. Frank checked his map.

"We're close to a danger zone marked on the map," he said. He read aloud. "There are symbols all over the place marking steep drops and rock slide areas. You don't think Rob—"

"Let's check it out," Joe cut in quickly. "If Rob's had a fall—or worse—he'll need help, and fast."

As the Hardys ran into the danger area, Joe understood immediately why runners had been warned off that area. Narrow ledges and deep drops, hidden by dense foliage, made even walking difficult. Small rocks gave way under their feet as they made their way along a steep ridge.

Reaching a narrow ledge on the steep mountainside, the exhausted brothers paused to reconnoiter. There was absolute quiet on the mountain, and Joe wondered how often that isolated spot had been visited by humans. The thought that they could be the first visitors in years disturbed him a little. He watched as Frank unfolded the map.

"According to this, the whole area around here is full of folds and niches," Frank muttered. "Rob could be anywhere—and if he's hurt, an entire search party might never find him."

"Then we'll have to," Joe retorted as he leaned over to check the map. But as he tried to decipher the many symbols, his concentration was broken by a cry in the forest.

"Hey! Someone help me!" Two faint voices cut through the silence.

Chapter

14

"DID YOU HEAR THAT?" Joe asked under his breath.

He and Frank stood perfectly still, straining to listen. Joe's heart was beating so fast he was afraid it would drown out any other sound.

"I heard it," Frank said. "I think it came from over there." He pointed back and to the right, where the mountainside was shrouded in a blanket of trees.

Without a word both brothers began running in that direction. As they reentered the thick forest, Joe tried to peer ahead through the dense growth but found it impossible to see more than half a dozen feet in any direction. The forest floor was littered with small rocks, making it difficult to run very fast.

"Help!" came another cry.

Frank and Joe hesitated, determining where the voice was coming from, then they sped ahead again in that direction. After pushing through a patch of wild raspberry canes and racing down a slight decline, Frank suddenly pulled up short.

"Ugh!" Joe grunted, slamming into Frank's back. "What gives?" Frank stepped aside so Joe could look down to see that they were on the edge of a deep crevice. It was as if a piece of the mountain had been cut away with a sharp knife. The wedge-shaped opening had lost most of its topsoil, and it was now a rocky, fifteen-foot drop to nowhere.

"Oh. Good decision to stop," Joe said to his brother, who had squatted beside the small canyon to catch his breath. Joe peered down the sheer side of the crevice and saw movement on its dimly lit floor. An instant later Joe managed to make out two figures standing at the bottom.

"It's Rob and Takashi!" he said to Frank. Both of the o-ers were covered with dirt, Joe saw as they stepped into a patch of sunlight. Neither looked very happy.

"Are you guys okay?" Joe yelled.

"Oh, sure," Rob called back up weakly. "I'd be fine if my head would stop pounding."

"What happened?" Frank asked, peering down at the two o-ers.

"I'll tell you what happened!" Takashi shouted

back up. "This idiot purposely tried to get me killed so I couldn't beat him."

Rob broke in, ignoring Takashi's accusation. "One minute I'm following the map, and the next minute this drop comes out of nowhere!"

"Yeah, right," Takashi said, turning to Rob. "You did this on purpose, you weasel. You're still mad at me for pushing you into that ditch in the Montana meet last fall."

"Give me a break," Rob said. "You're the one who's been shooting at me all week."

"Ha!" Takashi cried out in disbelief. "That's a good one—shooting at you. Nice imagination, Niles. Did you tell that one to the coach, too?"

"I don't think being shot at is all that funny," Rob said, sounding disgusted. "In fact, I'm sick of it. As soon as we get back to the starting line, I plan to report you to the officials."

"Hold on!" Frank yelled. "Let's get you out of there first." He turned to Joe. "We've got to find something to pull them up with," he said quietly, "before they start fighting."

The Hardys began a quick search of the area. Though Joe noticed a few small branches lying around, there wasn't anything long enough to reach Rob and Takashi. Just as Joe began to think he and Frank would have to come up with another plan, he spied a small pine tree that had been broken off at its base. The sapling must have fallen in a storm, Joe guessed. It was at least ten feet long.

133

Dragging the small tree back to the crevice, he called for Frank. "What do you think?" he said, motioning to the pine.

"Let's give it a shot," Frank said.

The Hardys lay side by side at the edge of the small canyon. Then they lowered the sapling over the sheer rock side, hanging on to the lower, thicker branches near the broken-off trunk. "Okay," Joe yelled to Rob and Takashi, "use this as a rope!"

"You got it," Rob called up.

"Out of my way!" Takashi shouted. "You got me into this, so I'm getting out first." Grabbing on to the tree, he began climbing up the rocky wall, planting his feet against the sheer side. As Frank and Joe strained against the athlete's weight, Takashi made his way to the top. Near the ledge he grasped Frank's arm and heaved himself up and over the top. Rob quickly followed.

Frank and Joe let go of the sapling and turned to Rob and Takashi, who were standing and fuming. "Are either of you hurt?" Frank asked.

"I think we're all right," Rob said, brushing dirt from his jumpsuit. Joe saw that he had a few scrapes on his face, but none of them was bleeding. "It's a good thing the college makes us wear all this protective gear when we run," Rob added.

"What happened?" Joe asked. "What were you two doing here?"

"What happened is that Rob led me off course on purpose." Takashi's eyes were flashing. "He heard me on his tail, so he made a turn at the last minute—right into this drop. My map fell when I did, and now I can't find it."

Rob's voice began to rise. "I didn't lead you off course. I was following the map. Besides, you know better than to follow a competitor. Not only is it against the rules, but it's just about the surest way to lose."

Takashi ripped Rob's map out of his hand. "I still have time to win this thing," he blurted out. Before the others could react, Takashi was racing back through the trees with Rob's map.

"Hey!" Rob shouted, taking off after Takashi. He stopped quickly. "Forget it," he said to the Hardys. "I've lost too much time, anyway."

"Take it easy," Frank said. "I still don't understand what you were doing in this area."

"What do you mean, 'this area'?" Rob snapped in frustration. "I followed a route that my map said would lead me to a short, dry creek bed. It should have been easy to jump over. Takashi was right on my heels, and we both got to what I thought was the creek bed at the same time. I was going so fast that I was just relying on the map without checking where my feet were going. Just as we jumped, I realized it was actually a gorge."

He paused for a moment, shaking his head. "We really are lucky to be alive. If some bushes

135

at the bottom hadn't broken our falls, we'd be history."

"But there isn't a control point around here," Frank said, puzzled. "In fact, the whole area is marked as a danger zone. You were way off course."

"No way," Rob protested hotly. "My map showed a control right over this ridge." He pointed down to the hill below. "At my level you don't make that kind of mistake," he told the Hardys. "The map showed a checkpoint. I'm positive."

"Look, Rob," Frank said. He had pulled out his own map and was pointing toward a spot on it. Rob bent over and studied it quickly. Then he looked up, a blank expression on his face.

"I don't get it," he said. He pointed to the next few circled numbers on Frank's map. "These points weren't even on my map. And some of my checkpoints went way up here," he said, pointing to a section that was marked as a danger zone.

"Are you sure?" Joe asked. "That could put you in serious danger."

Rob continued staring at the map. "I'm positive," he said firmly. "Some of the checkpoints are the same, but I know for sure the last one on my map is different. I'd have ended up going way to the side of you guys."

"And everybody else," Frank pointed out. He

and Joe lifted their heads from the map at the same time to exchange a quick glance.

"You got an altered map," Joe burst out.

Rob sputtered, "But—wha— Who?"

"Jeremy Foote," Frank said decisively.

"Jeremy?" Rob blanched.

"Frank thought he saw him running on the course earlier," Joe said. "He's obviously the one who's been after you."

"Are you sure?" Rob said, still trying to grasp the situation.

"Look, someone was trying to put you off course," Frank said excitedly, "and ultimately lead you to a different part of the area. An area where there'd be no other competitors," he added.

"So I'd lose," Rob finished.

"You might do more than just lose," Frank said simply. "If Jeremy was trying to draw you into the wilderness, I don't think he was just thinking about race results."

Rob suddenly understood. "I was being set up again," he said, panic registering in his voice. "I would have been an open target out here."

"Right," Joe cut in. "But not anymore. Now Takashi's the one with the altered map. He's just become the target!"

Chapter

15

"WE'VE GOT TO catch him," Joe said urgently.
"Who knows what Jeremy has waiting for him?
Let's go!"

"Hold on," Frank said, grabbing Joe's arm.
"Takashi's a top o-er—and he has a big head
start. There's no way we can overtake him."

"What about you, Rob?" Joe asked impatiently. "Do you think you can catch up to
Takashi?"

"If we cut through the middle of the course
and head straight for his final checkpoint, we
may beat him to it. That's if Jeremy plans to do
him in at the final checkpoint."

"Okay," Frank said. "But do you remember
where the last checkpoint on your fake map
was?"

Rob nodded. "I don't know the exact spot, but I know the general vicinity. It's a mile or so away if we cut straight through."

"Then what are we waiting for?" Joe said.

"Nothing. Follow me," Rob called back over his shoulder, already beginning to run.

Frank and Joe took off after Rob, who was sprinting down the mountainside, deftly dodging rocks and branches. After weaving in and out of the trees dotting the slope, Rob led them into a clearing, where they were able to sprint with few impediments.

The ground seemed to fly beneath Frank as he tried to keep up with Rob. He could see why Rob was a national champion. He picked his way through the wilderness swiftly and confidently, choosing the fastest routes instinctively and occasionally checking the compass attached to his wrist by a string.

After a few more minutes Rob slowed down and stopped. Frank and Joe came to a halt just behind him, breathing hard as they took stock of their surroundings. Joe could feel the effects of the high altitude. He felt winded and dizzy after a run he could have managed easily in Bayport. As he caught his breath, he studied the peaks and trees around them, noticing a tiny lake almost hidden by trees and brush. "I hope you know where we are," he said to Rob.

Rob pointed to a mountaintop straight ahead of them and checked his compass again. "I think the fake checkpoint is on that rounded peak there," he said. "Let's check your map again, Frank," he said, "and fast." Frank unfolded the official race map, and he and Rob studied it for a few moments.

Suddenly Joe grabbed Frank's shoulder. "Look!" he cried. "Running down that hill just ahead—isn't that Takashi?"

Frank and Rob jerked their heads up. Frank caught sight of a figure running down a hill to his right. As the figure weaved its way among the trees, Frank caught glimpses of an orange nylon jumpsuit, like the one Takashi had been wearing.

"Takashi!" Rob yelled out.

The man continued running. "He can't hear you," Joe said. "Besides, even if he could, he'd probably think we were just trying to sabotage him."

"But if Rob's right, and that peak up there is the last checkpoint, then Takashi's almost done," Frank said. "He just has to run through the valley below, and then up . . ." His voice trailed off as he stared up at the peak.

"What is it?" Joe said.

Frank squinted at the peak, a few hundred yards away. "There's someone up there," he said. "And if I'm not mistaken, it's Jeremy."

Joe and Rob followed Frank's gaze. Joe could see a man standing in a clearing on the ridge peak. He seemed to be shielding his eyes from the sun with one arm.

"That's Jeremy, all right," Rob said. They watched as Jeremy's other arm slowly rose in front of him.

"He has a rifle," Joe said in a flat voice. "He must be tracking Takashi."

Rob said, his own voice cracking a little, "Takashi and I are wearing the exact same jumpsuit—our team uniforms. From where Jeremy's standing, Takashi could look just like me."

"At any rate he'd think you'd be the only one this far off course," Frank pointed out. "You were supposed to be the only one with an altered map."

"Jeremy'll kill him!" Rob said.

"Not if we get there first," Joe said grimly.

"He's still quite a distance from us," Frank said. "We might not make it."

"Then what *do* we do?" Rob cut in.

"Can you catch Takashi?" Frank said to Rob.

Rob nodded. "I think so."

"Then do it. Get him to some cover. But be sure to stay out of Jeremy's line of sight when you go into the valley. Joe and I will go after Jeremy."

Rob nodded again. "Good luck," he said, taking off through the forest.

"What I said goes for us, too," Frank said to Joe. "We've got to find cover on our way up the hill."

"Got it," Joe said. He took off into the valley, veering to the right of Rob. He wouldn't waste time going all the way to the bottom of the valley when they could approach the mountain where Jeremy stood from the side. He could feel his heart thudding in his chest as he cut a path through the trees, with Frank close at his heels. He was pleading silently that they wouldn't hear the sound of a gunshot.

"Do you know where you're going?" Frank called from behind, his breath coming in gasps. Joe slowed so that he could run beside Frank. "I think so," he said. "We should be coming up the hill just behind Jeremy."

The climb became steeper, and Frank and Joe were forced to slow down. The still forest was silent except for the sound of their breathing and the occasional rustling of a bird or chipmunk. Joe's forehead was beaded with perspiration, and he could feel the strain in his leg muscles.

Finally they reached a level section of the mountain, a clearing that provided a view back down to the valley. Joe stole up carefully, staying back from the edge of the clearing. He could see, off to his right and just a bit farther up the mountain, Jeremy watching the valley below.

Staying behind the sole pine tree in the clearing, Joe peered down the mountain, training his eyes along the path he thought Rob must have taken. Scanning the valley, he suddenly caught sight of a flash of orange. In a space between two clumps of trees, a figure in a jumpsuit zipped by. It was Takashi.

Within seconds Joe saw another flash of orange in that same open space. He felt a moment's relief as he realized that Rob had nearly caught up with Takashi.

Just then he felt Frank grab at his shirt. He turned to see his brother pointing up the hill. Joe caught sight of Jeremy, who had moved and was now standing on a higher ledge off to the side of them. The ad executive had his rifle raised, aiming into the valley below.

Joe peered down the mountain. Takashi and Rob had just run into an open area. Rob, only a couple of feet behind Takashi, suddenly leapt toward his teammate and tackled him to the ground. The two orienteerers lay on the ground, completely open to those on the mountain.

In two strides Joe made it across the clearing. As he began the run up the ledge to where Jeremy stood, Jeremy whipped around and saw him. In the next instant Joe leapt the last foot and dived, ramming his shoulder into Jeremy's knees.

A gunshot rang out next to Joe's ear. For a moment Joe lost sight of Jeremy as the sound continued to echo inside his skull. On his knees he raised his head and saw Jeremy on the ground in front of him. The rifle lay between them. Joe quickly glanced down the mountain. Rob and Takashi were no longer in sight.

Jeremy was on his knees now, too, facing Joe. "Why, you little—" he began, glaring wildly at Joe. He dived for the rifle, and Joe sprung up to intercept him. He hit Jeremy's shoulders, and the two grappled. Joe tried to flip Jeremy to the ground, hoping to gain the upper hand, but Jeremy gripped the younger Hardy in a chokehold. He slammed Joe's head to the ground. From the corner of his eye, Joe saw Jeremy reach back with one arm to grab the rifle.

Just then Frank reached the ledge and began to charge Jeremy. The ad man had already gained control of the gun. "Don't even think about it," he spat out to Frank, panting.

Frank stopped and stood perfectly still, barely moving his eyes to glance at Joe, who was lying motionless on the ledge. Fear gripped him. He felt as if someone had just squeezed the air from his chest.

Jeremy's face was contorted in an expression of wild anger. Slowly he lifted the rifle to his shoulder, placing the barrel only inches from Frank's face.

He closed one eye to take aim. "Say goodbye to life, kid," he growled at Frank.

Chapter

16

FRANK STARED DOWN the barrel of the gun, not daring to move a muscle. The Jeremy who now held the gun wasn't the tidy professional Frank had first seen, but a wild-eyed madman. Every muscle in Frank's body was taut, and he could feel perspiration slowly trickle down his neck. His eyes were trained on Jeremy as he desperately tried to think of a way to disarm him.

Suddenly Joe brought his knees to his chest, and in the next instant he thrust his legs out, hitting Jeremy squarely in the knees. Jeremy's legs buckled beneath him, and the rifle flew out of his hands. Frank immediately jumped on top of Jeremy, pinning him to the ground. At the same time Joe sprang to his feet and grabbed the gun. He stood over Frank and Jeremy, who was still trying to wriggle away.

Joe pointed the rifle at Jeremy. "It's over," he said. "Give it up." Jeremy looked up at the rifle and turned back to Frank. His squirming stopped and he lay still. His contorted facial muscles relaxed, but he continued to glare at Frank.

"Are you okay?" Frank asked Joe.

Joe nodded. "I think I'll have a nice golf ball on the back of my head tomorrow," he said, "but I'm fine."

"Hey, Joe!" Joe spun around with the rifle to see Rob and Takashi climbing up the ledge. "Watch where you're pointing that thing, huh?" Rob said, eyeing the rifle nervously. Joe quickly dropped the gun to his side. Rob looked over at Jeremy. "Nice work, guys," he said to Frank and Joe.

Takashi was staring at Jeremy in astonishment. "So he really was trying to shoot me—or actually, you," he said to Rob.

"I told you," Rob said.

Takashi shook his head. "Hey, I'm sorry, Rob," he said. "I never would have grabbed that map from you if I had known—"

"Don't worry about it," Rob interjected. "There's no way any of us could have known. I'm just glad I got to you when I did."

Takashi clapped a hand on Rob's shoulder. "That makes two of us," he said gratefully.

Frank and Joe had pulled Jeremy to his feet.

"Let's get our friend here back down to the ranger station," Joe said, motioning to Jeremy. "I think he has some questions to answer."

"Yeah," Rob said quietly, facing Jeremy. "Like, why? Why would you want to kill me?" he asked.

"Don't pull your Mr. Innocent act on me, you lousy prima donna," Jeremy blurted out to Rob. With Frank and Joe holding him, the ad executive leaned toward Rob, his body trembling. "You've been gunning for my job from day one," he said. "It's not enough to be Daddy's little favorite, is it? You had to push me aside, too. Well, no way!" he continued, almost screaming now. "I'm not about to let some all-star jerk put one over on me."

Rob had been watching Jeremy, his eyes wide. "I wasn't trying to take over your job," he said, shaking his head. "I was supposed to work *for* you."

"Oh, please," Jeremy shot back. "I'm not an idiot. I know what that means. You and 'Daddy' were just trying to get rid of me. Quit being such a coward and admit it."

Rob still shook his head in amazement.

"Forget it," Frank said to him. "He obviously believes what he wants to believe."

"I believe the truth!" Jeremy yelled at Frank.

"Let's go," Frank said to Joe in disgust. Joe nodded, and the five of them started down the mountain, Joe carrying Jeremy's rifle and both Hardys clutching Jeremy between them.

After a few moments of silence Joe spoke up. "I guess I owe you an apology," he said to Takashi. "I mean, breaking into your room and everything. I really thought you were trying to hide something."

"Well," Takashi said, hesitating, "I was. I did type those warning notes to Rob," he admitted. "I borrowed a typewriter from the hotel."

"I *knew* it!" Rob said, almost stopping in his tracks.

"That was just standard psych-job stuff," Takashi defended himself. "But I do feel bad about the snake. I don't know what came over me."

"So *you* put the snake in Rob's room," Joe said. "And you know how much he hates them," he said, wondering about Takashi's motivation.

"Yeah, I do know," Takashi admitted. "That's why I feel bad."

"Where'd you get the snake?" Joe asked him. "We were hoping the animal control people would be able to trace it, but they never called us back."

"They wouldn't have been able to," Takashi said with a snort of derision. "A couple of guys on the team found it during a practice run the other day. We thought it'd give Rob a good scare."

"It did," Rob admitted.

"Well, I'm sorry I did it," Takashi said sincerely. "I guess I was just nervous about the nationals." He paused. "But I didn't tell Coach about you breaking into my room." Rob glanced at the Hardys and smiled.

"What I want to know is, why were you hanging around with Malika Morris?" Joe demanded. "It looked a little weird for an athlete to be lunching with the rival team's coach."

"I guess so," Takashi said. "But there was nothing weird about it. I was just asking Coach Morris about finding a corporate sponsor after I graduated. I knew she'd done it after college, and I wanted to find out how to go about it. Coach Morris has been looking for a job here in Idaho, so we talked about that, too."

"But you and Terence showed up at my photo shoot," Rob reminded him.

Takashi shrugged. "I wanted to see what an ad shoot is like in case I find a sponsor. I've known Terence for a few years, and we were both more than a little curious. That's all." He stopped walking for a moment. "You're not going to report me for following you on the course, are you? I know it's illegal. I was so crazy to beat you that I lost my head for a minute. When I saw you going a different way, I was sure you'd figured out a faster route. I can't believe I ignored the rule Coach Santina has been pounding into our heads for years: Never follow, always lead."

"Oh, spare me your coach's words of wisdom," Jeremy suddenly spit out, and twisted in Joe's grip.

Rob suddenly seemed to remember that Jeremy was there. He shook his head. "I can't believe it," he said quietly. "The whole time you've been here, you've been trying to kill me," he said.

Jeremy gave a short, bitter laugh and remained silent.

"This assignment was perfect for him—or so he thought," Frank said. "He followed us around, hoping to create an 'accident'—causing a rock slide, shooting out the raft on the Middle Fork, even shooting at you, Rob."

"So that was *your* visor Joe found during our o-ing run?" Rob asked Jeremy.

Jeremy glared at Rob, admitting nothing.

"And he rigged the photo shoot, too," Joe said. "There was no way he wanted to see Rob being featured in a national advertising campaign."

"But all along you knew that if none of that worked, you still had your ace in the hole, right?" Frank said to Jeremy.

"There was no way I could fail with this race," Jeremy muttered, shaking his head. "I had it all planned."

When he saw that Jeremy wasn't going to explain, Frank said, "My guess is that in those few days he spent in Idaho before he ran into Rob, he got hold of a map of the course and actually came out here to see how he could create a new, fake course."

"So *he* was the burglar at the o-ing club headquarters," Joe put in. "All he did was copy the map and leave."

"Right. And he changed our map a little, too, so we'd fall into that pit," Frank said. "Or was the pit your photographer's idea, Jeremy?"

The executive whipped his head around to look at Frank. "Andy had nothing to do with this. Nothing, do you hear me?" he said. "He's spent most of this trip taking nature shots. We've barely seen each other."

Joe looked at his brother. "I guess that's a confession—of sorts," he said.

"I still don't get it," Takashi said. "How could he make sure Rob and you would get the new map and fall into his trap?"

"He volunteered to help at the starting line, remember?" Rob told him. "You must have seen him there."

"That's right," Frank said. "He gave all three of us our maps—personally." He looked over at Jeremy to see if the executive was going to correct anything he'd said. Jeremy remained silent, scowling at the ground.

A few minutes later the group came within view of the observation tower. As they approached, Frank could see a small crowd of people milling about the foot of the tower. Suddenly Callie broke from the group and pointed toward

Frank and the others. A smile broke out on her face as she began to run toward Frank. Coach Santina followed.

Soon the two groups came together, with park rangers taking custody of Jeremy Foote. Frank and Callie exchanged a hug and race officials rushed up to tend to Takashi and Rob. Joe handed the rifle over to the rangers, and then joined Frank, Callie, and Liz.

"Thank goodness you're all right," Callie said to Frank and Joe. "When Malika radioed the tower to say that you guys had been looking for Rob, and that they hadn't seen him, we were frantic."

"So Jeremy Foote was behind all this?" Liz asked in surprise, scribbling in her notebook as she watched Jeremy being led away.

Frank nodded. "He said Rob was trying to push him out of his job. He figured that Rob's dad would simply let Rob take over all of Jeremy's accounts."

"And he was pretty angry about the favoritism he thought Rob was getting," Joe added. "Even though Rob said his father had no intention of handing him Jeremy's job."

"So Jeremy decided to *kill* Rob?" Callie asked in disbelief. "That's pretty warped."

"He thought the only way to save his own career was to end Rob's," Frank explained.

Just then Frank felt a tap on his shoulder. He turned to find Malika Morris standing in front of him. "I've just been listening to Rob and Takashi explain what happened to them," she said. "I'm glad you two were around. Whether or not you believe it, I would never want anything to happen to either of them."

Joe smiled. "I know that now," he said. "But I've been wondering—that *was* you and Terence out on the course that day when I was yelling for help, right?"

Malika nodded. "I'm glad neither of you was hurt badly. Terence and I had just realized that we had mistakenly wandered onto an embargoed part of the course. We started to run over to help, but then I got worried that someone would find out we were there and think we were cheating. I *am* sorry," she added.

Frank nodded. "But what about those compasses?" he said. "Did you really give them to the club knowing they wouldn't work?"

Malika's face colored a bit. "No," she said, shaking her head emphatically. "But I should have known. I just didn't even think about it. I'd been carrying those compasses around with me, and I was glad to think the club could use them. But when Rob confronted me, I was totally taken aback," she said. "I knew there was no way he'd believe me if I said I had forgotten about that southern hemisphere thing. I know it sounds lame," she said, rolling her eyes, "but it's the truth."

"What's lame is the way I lashed out without

thinking," a voice said behind her. The group turned to see Rob, a big smile on his face and his hand wrapped in Sylvia's. Coach Santina hovered behind him, obviously relieved.

"Sorry, Coach Morris—I've just been feeling a little like a hunted animal these past few days," Rob said to the woman. "I've lost count of the near misses we had."

"I have to apologize, too, Malika," Coach Santina said to her. "When we began having suspicions, I should have talked to you directly, like a professional."

As the rival coaches shook hands, Rob turned to the Hardys. "And thanks again for your help, guys. I think I'm figuring out that there are a few things more important than o-ing." He glanced at Sylvia with a twinkle in his eye.

"Well, it looks like I've been pretty lucky, too," Sylvia said as Liz stepped back to take a picture of the entire group.

"Thanks, all of you, for saving this guy," Sylvia said to her new friends. Then she laughed. "I guess you could say I *o* you!"

Frank and Joe's next case:

A sophisticated ring of luggage thieves has put a choke hold on Eddings Air, threatening to ground the young airline for good. Working undercover as baggage handlers, the Hardys agree to scope out the airline's center of operations in Atlanta. But their welcome is less than cordial—Frank and Joe discover that they too may be headed for a crash landing!

From the complex of tunnels beneath the airport to the enigmatic pasts of the airline's employees, the boys are drawn into a labyrinth of sabotage and deceit. Picking up clues to a conspiracy extending far beyond a few missing suitcases, they begin to suspect that much more than the future of Eddings Air is at stake. A scheme is in place, a plot about to unfold, in which murder is only the beginning . . . in *Tagged for Terror*, Case #76 in The Hardy Boys Casefiles™ and the first adventure in the Ring of Evil Trilogy.

THE HARDY BOYS® CASE FILES

☐	#1: DEAD ON TARGET	73992-1/$3.75		
☐	#2: EVIL, INC.	73668-X/$3.75		
☐	#3: CULT OF CRIME	68726-3/$3.75		
☐	#4: THE LAZARUS PLOT	73995-6/$3.75		
☐	#5: EDGE OF DESTRUCTION	73669-8/$3.50		
☐	#6: THE CROWNING OF TERROR	73670-1/$3.50		
☐	#7: DEATHGAME	73993-8/$3.50		
☐	#8: SEE NO EVIL	73673-6/$3.50		
☐	#9: THE GENIUS THIEVES	73767-4/$3.50		
☐	#10: HOSTAGES OF HATE	69579-7/$2.95		
☐	#11: BROTHER AGAINST BROTHER	74391-0/$3.50		
☐	#12: PERFECT GETAWAY	73675-2/$3.50		
☐	#13: THE BORGIA DAGGER	73676-0/$3.50		
☐	#14: TOO MANY TRAITORS	73677-9/$3.50		
☐	#15: BLOOD RELATIONS	68779-4/$2.95		
☐	#16: LINE OF FIRE	68805-7/$2.95		
☐	#17: THE NUMBER FILE	68806-5/$2.95		
☐	#18: A KILLING IN THE MARKET	68472-8/$2.95		
☐	#19: NIGHTMARE IN ANGEL CITY	69185-6/$2.95		
☐	#20: WITNESS TO MURDER	69434-0/$2.95		
☐	#21: STREET SPIES	69186-4/$2.95		
☐	#22: DOUBLE EXPOSURE	69376-X/$2.95		
☐	#23: DISASTER FOR HIRE	70491-5/$2.95		
☐	#24: SCENE OF THE CRIME	69377-8/$2.95		
☐	#25: THE BORDERLINE CASE	72452-5/$2.95		
☐	#26: TROUBLE IN THE PIPELINE	74661-8/$3.50		
☐	#27: NOWHERE TO RUN	64690-7/$2.95		
☐	#28: COUNTDOWN TO TERROR	74662-6/$3.50		
☐	#29: THICK AS THIEVES	74663-4/$3.50		
☐	#30: THE DEADLIEST DARE	74613-8/$3.50		
☐	#31: WITHOUT A TRACE	74664-2/$3.50		
☐	#32: BLOOD MONEY	74665-0/$3.50		
☐	#33: COLLISION COURSE	74666-9/$3.50		
☐	#34: FINAL CUT	74667-7/$3.50		
☐	#35: THE DEAD SEASON	74105-5/$3.50		
☐	#36: RUNNING ON EMPTY	74107-1/$3.50		
☐	#37: DANGER ZONE	73751-1/$3.75		
☐	#38: DIPLOMATIC DECEIT	74106-3/$3.50		

☐	#39: FLESH AND BLOOD	73913-1/$3.50
☐	#40: FRIGHT WAVE	73994-8/$3.50
☐	#41: HIGHWAY ROBBERY	70038-3/$3.50
☐	#42: THE LAST LAUGH	74614-6/$3.50
☐	#43: STRATEGIC MOVES	70040-5/$2.95
☐	#44: CASTLE FEAR	74615-4/$3.75
☐	#45: IN SELF-DEFENSE	70042-1/$3.75
☐	#46: FOUL PLAY	70043-X/$3.75
☐	#47: FLIGHT INTO DANGER	70044-8/$3.75
☐	#48: ROCK 'N' REVENGE	70033-2/$3.50
☐	#49: DIRTY DEEDS	70046-4/$3.50
☐	#50: POWER PLAY	70047-2/$3.50
☐	#51: CHOKE HOLD	70048-0/$3.50
☐	#52: UNCIVIL WAR	70049-9/$3.50
☐	#53: WEB OF HORROR	73089-4/$3.50
☐	#54: DEEP TROUBLE	73090-8/$3.50
☐	#55: BEYOND THE LAW	73091-6/$3.50
☐	#56: HEIGHT OF DANGER	73092-4/$3.50
☐	#57: TERROR ON TRACK	73093-2/$3.50
☐	#58: SPIKED!	73094-0/$3.50
☐	#59: OPEN SEASON	73095-9/$3.50
☐	#60: DEADFALL	73096-7/$3.75
☐	#61: GRAVE DANGER	73097-5/$3.75
☐	#62: FINAL GAMBIT	73098-3/$3.75
☐	#63: COLD SWEAT	73099-1/$3.75
☐	#64: ENDANGERED SPECIES	73100-9/$3.75
☐	#65: NO MERCY	73101-7/$3.75
☐	#66: THE PHOENIX EQUATION	73102-5/$3.75
☐	#67: LETHAL CARGO	73103-0/$3.75
☐	#68: ROUGH RIDING	73104-1/$3.75
☐	#69: MAYHEM IN MOTION	73105-X/$3.75
☐	#70: RIGGED FOR REVENGE	73106-8/$3.75
☐	#71: REAL HORROR	73107-6/$3.75
☐	#72: SCREAMERS	73108-4/$3.75
☐	#73: BAD RAP	73109-2/$3.99
☐	#74: ROAD PIRATES	73110-6/$3.99
☐	#75: NO WAY OUT	73111-4/$3.99

Simon & Schuster Mail Order
200 Old Tappan Rd., Old Tappan, N.J. 07675

Please send me the books I have checked above. I am enclosing $_____ (please add $0.75 to cover the postage and handling for each order. Please add appropriate sales tax). Send check or money order—no cash or C.O.D.'s please. Allow up to six weeks for delivery. For purchase over $10.00 you may use VISA: card number, expiration date and customer signature must be included.

Name _____

Address _____

City _____ State/Zip _____

VISA Card # _____ Exp.Date _____

Signature _____ 762